City of Vengeance

By

Lisa Parkinson

All the best !
With love...
Lisa Parkinson

Beachfront

PRESS

Easton, PA

BEACHFRONT PRESS

FIRST EDITION, JUNE 2012

Parkinson, Lisa

City of Vengeance/ Lisa Parkinson

ISBN: 978-0-9881172-0-4

Author photo © 2011 Lisa Parkinson

For the wonderful boys in my life:

This dream could never have become a reality without

your unbridled love and support.

Thank you, Blain, Joshua, Nathan and Tristan.

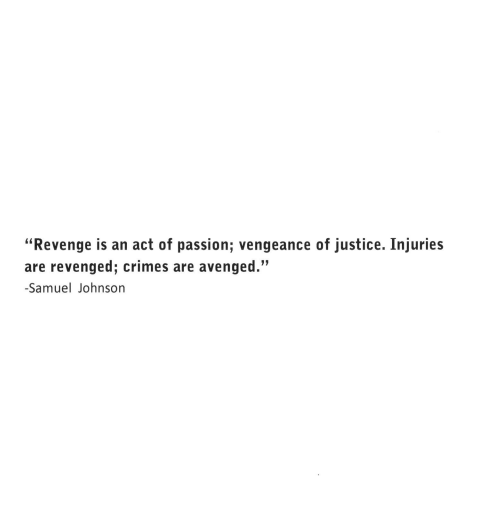

"Revenge is an act of passion; vengeance of justice. Injuries
are revenged; crimes are avenged."
-Samuel Johnson

CHAPTER ONE

Down on his knees, with his head drawn back, he looked heavenward as if to beg God for his life. He felt the cold, steel gun muzzle against his temple as a bead of sweat raced down his cheek. After years as one of the most prolific drug suppliers in New York City, this was how it was going to end. The cocking of the gun beside his ear seemed to fill the still streets.

His past life and impending doom played out against faint memories. The turf wars had heightened, and the Falcone family of New York wanted him to know who owned these streets. This dark September night had started like any other, with business taking place on the streets as usual. His right hand man, Frank, had set up a buy with Mexican suppliers, who had insisted on meeting with him directly. Frank had worked with the Mexican for years and his judgment and intuition were trusted. Lou Manendo was about to be proven wrong.

On this particular night, something wasn't right. A sense of foreboding hung in the air, and sent a chill down Lou's spine as the two met. His mind told him to run, but it was as if his body knew it was already too late. He was already surrounded by three, enormous, towering men: the supplier, some goon he didn't recognize—and Frank. He had been set up. Frank had been double-dealing, working for his chief rival, Tony Falcone. His heart raced as he realized he wouldn't be able to warn his son Joey and the boys.

Though Lou usually made certain to be out and about with his boys, Tony had caught him off guard. Lou and Tony had fought for these sordid streets for years, and finally one of them had made a fatal mistake. This was how it was going to end: betrayal, and Tony's drug minions winning the turf war.

Gunshots rang out in the alley, like someone had lit firecrackers.

Behind a large dumpster that sat in the parking lot adjacent to the alley, Marcus Leoni crouched, unnoticed, holding his breath. He knew that these thugs would never allow a witness to survive. Having grown up in these parts had taught Marcus many things: keep your head down, talk to no one, and mind your business. If you kept to each of these 'rules', you would have a better chance of surviving until you could get out.

Unlike most, Marcus was close to getting out. He had just been hired as an emergency room doctor by Centennial Memorial Hospital in Central Florida. In fact, Marcus had managed to graduate from medical school and do his medical internships in city hospitals. But he wasn't planning on working in the city forever. No, he wanted a better life than his family and friends had had.

He only had six more days left in this crime-ridden hell hole before he was to start his new life.

Ironically, Marcus had been on his way to pick up plane tickets at a neighbourhood travel agency.

It was on this walk that he had noticed a dark Escalade with its headlights off. It had slowly cruised alongside him and then swung into the next alley.

He had seen this sort of thing before, and knew instantly what was about to go down. He stopped dead in his tracks and suddenly turned and began to sprint through the used car lot to his right, in hopes of getting out of the line of fire. He heard the altercation in the alley start to heat up, and quickly ducked behind an overflowing dumpster.

Having witnessed the execution-style murder of a well-known drug pusher, Marcus' only chance for survival was to sit tight.

The approaching footsteps set him on edge. His blood ran cold. He dared not move. *Can they see me?* It was too late. All of his dreams of a better life faded to black as he turned to face his executioner, who pulled the trigger with extreme prejudice, shattering Marcus' skull.

CHAPTER TWO

The *New York Times* obituary read: "Beloved son, brother, friend and doctor, Marcus Leoni, was fatally shot on Wednesday – the unfortunate victim of another random crime on our sad streets. It is with heavy hearts that we bury Marcus at the Holy Cross Cemetery on Saturday at 9:00am. Please join the family in saying a final goodbye to this cherished and dear New Yorker."

Above the notice was a handsome photo of Marcus dressed in hospital scrubs, a stethoscope draped around his neck. His light brown hair, short on the sides and back, but with a longer, bed head style on top and in front, made him look like a Perry Ellis model at New York Fashion Week. His green eyes sparkled and his smile was as broad as always, including the dimple that always gave him such an innocent and warm attractiveness. The picture was both flattering and heartbreaking.

Tony Falcone looked at the obituary with complete satisfaction. Eyeballing Marcus' picture, and wagging his index finger, he proclaimed, "You were in the wrong place at the wrong time, buddy."

On the other side of downtown, Joey Manendo, son of Lou Manendo, was looking at the same newspaper page. *Why did you have to get caught?* Joey thought, then balling his fist in anger. "You saw dad die at Tony's hands. You would have been the perfect witness to put that bastard away," he anguished. "I guess it's up to me now to avenge dad's death."

The Saturday morning sun shone brilliantly as a gentle breeze swept through the cemetery.

"Beloved son, brother and friend, Marcus will be sadly missed, but we can rejoice in knowing that he is now with our Father in eternal Heaven."

Father Dominic stepped back from the freshly dug plot. The afternoon sun seemed to play with the chrome rails on the sides of Marcus' cherry-wood coffin.

Marcus' mother, the heart of this traditional Italian-American family, fell to her knees in anguish, reaching her hand out toward the coffin, as if half expecting her son would reach back. She wished so desperately that she could pull him away from his final fate. As if taking her cue, the core of the family and friends who still stood on either side of the burial plot wept in agony. The thought of never seeing Marcus' smile again seemed unbearable.

Then family members assisted the Leoni matriarch to her feet. They steadied her, like pillars of strength, so she could bid her son one final, composed goodbye.

The Priest added an appropriate, personalized comment, followed by the antiphon:

"As we now say our silent farewells to Marcus, keep us mindful, Heavenly Father, that he will always be present in our hearts, minds and souls – never to be forgotten."

Father Dominic stepped forward, while referencing Christ, "*I am the Resurrection and the Life,*" as the coffin was slowly lowered into the grave and the benediction recited. He started the first words of the Lord's Prayer, allowing the observant to finish silently. After sprinkling holy water on the coffin, he offered a final prayer: "Grant this mercy, O Lord, we beseech Thee, to Thy servant departed, that he may not receive in punishment the requital of his deeds who in desire did keep Thy will, and as the true faith here united him to the company of the faithful, so may Thy mercy unite him above to the choirs of angels, through Jesus Christ our Lord. Amen."

Marcus' immediate family, including his brother Gabe and his pregnant wife Theresa, younger sisters Mary and Franca, and his parents Anna and Joseph, then led the mourners to the awaiting line of limousines. Anguished wails could still be heard behind them as they filed into the awaiting cars, on their way back to the family home for an intimate reception.

Back at the family home, the sombre atmosphere reflected the life of a well-liked and sadly missed family member. Marcus' mom bravely sat in an over-sized leather armchair, systematically receiving the condolences of family and friends as they entered the house. "Anna, I'm so sorry for your loss," whispered many of the guests. "Thank you," Anna replied, as she received their kisses of respect, one on each cheek. The day was a complete blur. All Anna could think about was her little boy that had just been taken from her senselessly. A series of memories of Marcus as he grew up over the years from curious, troublesome boy to distinguished doctor, flooded her mind and became overwhelming. "Marcus…" she moaned, as she slumped to the floor in a wave of darkness. A fainting spell brought on by sheer heartache of never seeing her beloved son again.

CHAPTER THREE

Each air bubble ascended slowly to the surface with a peacefulness and grace. They emerged into the harbour air, rupturing blissfully.

The fall evening air was chilly, and the group of men now standing on the remote dock overlooking the river were anxious to get back into their warm vehicles. The silence was only broken by the sporadic sounds of surging air bubbles rising in the waters from the oil drum they had just dropped into the river.

They stood mute watching the drum sink to the bottom and praying silently for the demons to never resurface. It was a longstanding mafia tradition practiced in Italy for centuries.

One of their own men, someone who had pledged complete allegiance and loyalty to this family, had succumbed to the temptation of money offered by a rival drug family. Getting caught playing both sides is a death sentence, but this man had foolishly decided that it was worth the risk.

The Manendo family wasn't stupid. They sniffed out this rat that had been secretly working for their main rivals, the Falcones, and gunned him down as he sat on his front porch, kicking back with his nightly shot of Zambucca.

After putting a bullet in this traitor's head, two thugs had slipped out of a black sedan and dragged his lifeless body down the front steps onto the sidewalk below. These guys knew the drill, and moved with robotic ease. The driver had already made his way to the trunk of the vehicle, removed a faded, stained blue tarp, and proceeded to systematically unfold it and spread it out onto the street. The lifeless body was then lifted onto the tarp in one swift motion. The driver then enfolded the body by tucking it across the other side. The driver then flipped the body over several times, rolling it into the tarp as the other two gathered the ends and applied duct tape. All three men then picked up what looked like an enormous roll of limp Atlantic City taffy and tossed it in the trunk.

Next, the driver removed three neatly folded black handkerchiefs that were tucked into the front corner of the trunk and handed them to his colleagues. As each man stood stoically at the back of the car with the trunk now closed, they each proceeded to cleanse their hands of the traitor's blood.

A crisp breeze whistled through the night and rustled the heaps of decaying leaves that had accumulated along the curb of the street. One of the men pulled a large Ziploc bag from his back pocket and collected the soiled handkerchiefs. Closing the bag, he reminded himself to drop the bag off at Zio Michael's Dry Cleaning shop in the morning. The three men got back into the car and sped down the street. The two older women who had been sitting together on the porch across the street from the scene slowly rose from their chairs, grabbed their coffee mugs off the railing of the veranda, and went back inside the house. The show was over. Tomorrow evening they would resume their positions on the veranda, coffee in hand, and await the next round of entertainment.

The black sedan sped through the dark city streets towards the Hudson River Docks. One block east of the docks was a public storage facility in which the family owned and operated through alias names and friends. One of those units contained the equipment that would be needed to continue disposing of the corpse. The sedan slowed down when it approached the entrance gates and the driver gave a faint wave to the security guard positioned in the booth. A cloud of dust rose from behind the car as the tires spun in the gravel and the driver sped onto the lot. Conveniently located on the far side of the lot, this unit was considered off-limits to all personnel. Only the three men in the dark sedan had the key to access the unit – they were considered the eliminators of the family and this was their workshop.

The car pulled up in front of the unit and the driver put it in park as the front passenger got out and unlocked the large door. He grasped the bottom of the heavy door and heaved it upwards towards the sky. Standing off to the side, he watched as the driver reversed the car into the over-sized unit. Once the front end had cleared, he proceeded to reach up to the dangling chain on the bottom of the door and with one swift motion, pulled the garage door down until it slammed against the pavement. Over the course of the next two hours, the body would then be severed into smaller portions and packed into an awaiting oil drum. The cement would then be mixed and slowly poured into the drum to encase the body and add weight to the coffin - a final resting place for a disloyal conspirator.

The men now stood silently at the end of the dock, waiting impatiently for the drum to settle at the bottom of the river. This ritual was an extremely important part of life to the mafia-style Italian families in general. Italians, like many other European cultures, are very superstitious. By encasing the body in cement and disposing of it in a watery grave, meant that the spirit of the dead would no longer be able to rise and haunt the family in the future. It ensured that they could move forward with their operations, and not be bothered by stalking apparitions.

The hour had passed by relatively slowly for the men. Then, with a definitive nod from the leader of the group, they each turned around and walked back along the dock towards their awaiting car. The night had been a success. Tomorrow they would continue to exact their revenge against the Falcone members who had ruthlessly executed their leader, Lou Manendo the previous night. Anyone involved with that rival group would suffer. The family was in chaos now, and the family members scrambled to exact revenge on anyone and everyone involved.

CHAPTER FOUR

Marcus began to open his eyes as the white lights started to brighten into his sight. He slowly scanned the room for any sense of familiarity. The walls were a faded shade of white, with stains and markings outlining the years of distress in what appeared to be a well-used trauma centre. It was now ten days after the shooting incident, and Marcus was trying to figure out where he was and what had happened to bring him there.

Oh my God, the pain in my head, he thought, as he groaned and slowly moved his hand up to the back of his head. He could feel the outline of a thick gauze bandage taped to the back of his neck and up onto the lower part of his skull.

At that moment, a stream of doctors and nurses came flooding into the hospital room where Marcus had been laying in a coma since he was brought in. Monitors beeped incessantly as the doctors feverishly started to examine Marcus. It was the miracle that they had all been praying for. Not only had this man survived being shot at point-blank range in the back of the head, but also he was managing to put together basic phrases and slowly moving posterior limbs. "Where am I?" he asked a passing nurse, but the rush to check his vital statistics far exceeded the need to answer his questions at that point.

Security had been extremely tight at the hospital over the past ten days. When it was realized by emergency room doctors at that time, that they were saving the life of a mafia-hit witness, the flurry of activity became overwhelming. Local and federal authorities, outlining the extreme need for secrecy regarding this newest patient, called hospital management meetings.

As far as anyone not directly involved with the care of this patient was to know, Marcus had been fatally shot by an unknown assailant. He was pronounced dead shortly after arrival at the emergency room.

He was just another New York City citizen caught in the deadly crossfire of the streets.

What hospital staff and general public did not actually know was that within an hour after arrival at the trauma centre, his body was moved to a remote room in an older wing of the hospital, which had been phased out of service over the past few months while waiting for renovation.

Another local man, one of New York City's victims of homelessness, had also been checked into the emergency room about two hours prior to Marcus' arrival. The homeless man had run across some bad luck over the recent years and was drowning his sorrows that night with a bottle of Jack on the abandoned scaffolding of a partly demolished building. After staggering to his feet, the unstable structure of the scaffold began to sway, and the man was thrown off, impaling himself by the neck on a spiked railing that surrounded the property. After being found by another homeless man in the area, the patient was rushed to the emergency room with severe blood loss and obvious neck and head trauma. He was pronounced dead shortly before 8:00 pm.

Marcus, who arrived at 9:57 pm, was placed into the undisclosed location and his body replaced in the emergency room with that of the homeless man. With the same shades of light brown hair, and approximately the same fit build, it was not hard to assume that his body could be that of Marcus. With both of them suffering head and neck trauma, the homeless man's face had been visually unidentifiable - bloodied and broken enough to pass as that of Marcus. Two men, from different worlds, were to collide in fate - one not so fortunate to survive, and the other now fighting for recovery and security.

As the team of specialists continued over the next few days to perform testing on Marcus, a young surgeon named Dr. Paul Biasi, accompanied by Special Agent Tom O'Brien of the FBI, came to Marcus' bedside. Although Marcus had tried many times to get answers about what had happened to him, everyone seemed to avoid addressing the subject with him. Dr. Biasi and Agent O'Brien were now ready to give Marcus the answers he was searching for.

"You've been in a coma, Marcus. No one knows exactly what happened to you the night you were brought in, but you were admitted into Emergency with a single gunshot wound to the back of your skull. After rushing you into emergency surgery, our best team of surgeons managed to remove the bullet and stray fragments from the base of your skull. Fortunately for you, the bullet didn't get close enough to your brain to cause any brain-function damage, but you did receive some injury to the nerves and arteries at the base of your skull. With all the blood loss, we weren't even sure if you would survive the night, yet alone recover as much as you have," the doctor informed him.

Marcus lay there, stunned. After a few moments of silence, the Agent continued to prod his memory of that night.

"Do you remember anything about that night, Marcus? Any details to help us piece together what exactly happened?"

"I remember I was on my way to pick up my plane tickets from the travel agency on 5th Street. I was walking on the sidewalk, when I noticed a dark SUV with tinted windows driving really slowly past me. When it got about a block ahead, it then sped up and turned into an alley behind the old distillery."

Marcus turned his head away from the Agent, not wanting him to see the fear in his eyes as he remembered the feeling of panic that had shot through his body at that point.

"I started to run. I knew something really bad was going to go down. I ducked into the used car lot, and tried to find some place to hide – but the lights in the lot were so bright. I spotted a dumpster at the end of the lot and crouched low behind it."

"I heard gunshots and some guys yelling. I had tried to stay quiet so they wouldn't know I was there, but the shots were so loud that it scared me and made me lose my balance and my foot kicked the dumpster. I knew they were coming for me next. I closed my eyes and said a prayer."

"The next thing I know, I'm lying down in the back seat of a car and see a guy driving, looking back at me. I think I was drifting in and out of consciousness that whole time. Then I remember laying on a gurney and seeing the same guy walking down the hallway…he had a slight limp. I can't remember anything else after that."

Marcus turned back to look at the Agent and doctor, now sitting in chairs at his bedside. They each gave him a look of compassion and disbelief.

It was at that moment that Marcus felt an overwhelming need to know whom the unidentified guy with the limp was - the angel who must have saved him that cold, September night.

"Excuse me, Dr. Biasi," interrupted a nurse. "You're needed right away in the O.R." she stated.

Marcus turned his head and stared out the hospital room window. The sun was just beginning to set and the brilliant hues of orange and red streams were now piercing through his window and across the floor at the end of his bed. So what does this all mean for me now, he wondered with most uncertainty?

CHAPTER FIVE

Marcus shot straight up in his hospital bed. "What do you mean, Witness Protection? Are you serious?"

"Marcus, it's your only option if you ever want to live any sort of normal life again." Agent O'Brien tried to explain to him.

"What you witnessed was a drug hit between rival drug 'families'. The Falcone Family put the hit out on the leader of the Manendo Family, Lou Manendo. When they shot Lou, one of the lookout guys heard you move behind the dumpster. They are the ones who shot you in the back of the head."

"You were extremely lucky that there was also another witness to the murder nearby, but was not seen by the Falcones. He's the one who brought you to the hospital," the Agent explained.

"We have been trying to break up these rival drug families for years. With you as a star witness, now is our chance. When you were brought in and we were told what you had just witnessed, we realized instantly that you were the one and only person that could help us shut them down. The doctors have been working overtime to make sure that you not only survived, but also were in total isolation without anyone knowing you were still alive. We've been working extremely close with the hospital personnel to keep your status out of the media."

Marcus, trying to comprehend everything the Agent was saying, slowly leaned back against his hospital bed.

"What about my family?"

"Your family was contacted when you came in, but were told that you had been shot during a robbery attempt and succumbed to your injuries upon arrival at the emergency room. It was too risky to tell even your family what had really happened—or that you actually survived. It would have put a target on their backs. Your family thinks they have buried you. No one knows you are here, let alone alive. We want the Falcones to think they killed you that night. We even went as far as posting an obituary ad in the New York Times announcing your death and giving the funeral itinerary."

The Agent sat down on the chair next to his bedside.

"The doctors say you should be stable enough to get out of here in the next few days. You're still going to need to take care of your bandage, but the doctors will talk to you more about that before you leave. You'll be going into a witness protection program in Canada. A team of FBI agents, including myself, has been meeting with Canadian RCMP officers in Ottawa over the past week to arrange the cross-border transfer. The Canadian government has made special provisions for this program because of the intense scale of drug and crime activity that has been affecting their cities, too. You'll be going to a remote location in the Rocky Mountains until we can gather the evidence we need to arrest and prosecute the Falcones and Manendos." he explained.

"We'll set you up with a place to stay, money, clothes, and a new identity. It's just temporary until the District Prosecutor can secure their attempted murder case against the Falcones and we go to trial. The D.A. is hoping that once this happens that they may be able to get one of Tony's guys to accept a plea deal in exchange for dirt on Joey Manendo and their dealings. If that happens, then the Prosecutor can go after Manendo and we'll be able to get all of these guys off the streets and into jail."

"You'll be able to see your family and move on with your life at that point. Can you help us, Marcus?"

Marcus turned his head and stared intently out the hospital room window. The birds floating past his window suddenly seemed to exude such freedom. "Do I have a choice?" Marcus murmured sarcastically under his breath.

~~cooஇ✷ிௐoo~~

"Now Marcus, your wound is still relatively fresh," Dr. Biasi informed him as Marcus sat on the edge of his hospital bed, dressed in a pair of jeans and a t-shirt provided to him by the FBI.

"I'm going to put together a bag for you that will have some things you're going to need to take care of that wound. Twice a day, I want you to put the antibiotic cream on the incision where we took out the bullet fragments. Put on fresh bandages each time to keep it clean. I've also provided you with some Tylenol 3's for the pain. You may find that you'll experience headache pain more frequently, originating from the nerves at the back of your neck that were damaged. The Tylenol will help that."

"In about a week, you can take the bandage off and let the wound get some air to heal it. The stitches are dissolvable from the inside so the scarring should be minimal."

Marcus reached out and took the medical package that the doctor was now handing him.

"Thanks."

The awaiting Agent leaned over and helped Marcus slowly get off his bed. Marcus was then led through a back hospital entrance to a waiting black sedan. His journey was about to begin.

CHAPTER SIX

As the plane took off, Marcus stared longingly out the window. This is definitely not where I thought I'd be this week, he thought. He reflected on the surgeon position he was supposed to have started in Florida last week. I'm supposed to be working in the hospital and then lying on the beach on my days off, he thought grudgingly. With an overwhelming feeling of sudden resentment, he quickly reached behind his neck and gently pulled off the bandage. Placing the bandage, still damp with antibiotic cream, into his pocket, he reached back to the wound once again. He slowly ran his fingers across the two-inch long scab that was now starting to form on the back of his neck. I refuse to keep this bandage on to remind me of the shooting, he thought.

As he lay back in his seat, he started to think about the family he now left behind. His parents - they must be heartbroken. My brother and sisters must be beside themselves trying to comfort them. Although we had a pretty tough upbringing, our family managed to stay tight throughout the years. My brother Gabe was always the life of the party. He hung around with some really tough crowds in high school though. He's done well for himself since then, Marcus thought. He's now married to Theresa, and they are expecting their first child. Dad is so excited about his first grandchild! Gabe getting that job at the warehouse down by the shipping docks was good for him and his family. At least they could start saving up for their new baby.

Then there's Mary - fresh out of college with a degree in business administration. After Mary found a job, she and her boyfriend, Paulo, were going to get an apartment.

And then there's the baby of the family – Franca. She just started her last year of high school this month. A popular cheerleader with many friends, she seems to have the world at her feet. She was going to be okay, he thought.

They'll all be okay eventually. But it will be hard for them to get through the next few months…maybe years. Who knows how long I will be in this program, away from them all. Marcus miserably looked to the heavens and made a plea to God to help him and his family during this life-shattering time.

Although lost in thought about his family and life growing up, Marcus suddenly felt drawn to look out the airplane window again. The sun was beginning to rise up over the snow-capped mountain range of the Rocky Mountains. The sun reflecting on the fresh, powdered snow, made each snowflake glisten with peace and serenity as it danced across the mountainside with each sweep of wind that picked it up.

This was going to be his new home for a while. The FBI had told him that he was going to be put up in a lodge in Kananaskis, Alberta, Canada, located between Calgary and Banff. He sighed and resigned himself to the fact that it was definitely not going to be like New York City, but maybe he'd get used to the wildlife and natural outdoor setting that he'd never experienced before.

And with that thought, the plane slowly started its descent into the Calgary International Airport. Both serene and electric, this city boasted large skyscrapers and corporate offices found in the downtown core, surrounded by residential communities nestled just in the foothills of the mountains.

With a slight nudge from the FBI agent sitting beside him, Marcus snapped back into his reality, tightened his seat belt and closed his eyes. He just sat still and let the feeling of the plane's descent carry him towards his new life that now awaited him. The journey was to begin for Dr. Marcus Leoni.

CHAPTER SEVEN

As the black sedan slowly pulled out of the airport passenger pick-up lane, Marcus sadly gazed out the window once again. He tried to take in as much of the Calgary city scenery as he could before they were on the long road leading out towards the mountains - which from the sights of the city seemed incredibly miniature in the distance.

Over the next hour, Marcus managed to close his eyes and nap somewhat. Although he stirred frequently, it was just the refresher he needed after such a long trip. When he finally opened his eyes towards the end of their journey, he suddenly found himself barely able to catch his breath.

The enormous mountains that had now surrounded them became overwhelming. They stood tall, almost proud, casting both shadows and sun streams all around the car. The snow glistened in the evening sunset on the heavenly mountaintops. Surrounded at their bases by forests of gold, red and orange, the views became unspeakably breathtaking. It was as if God felt bad for the position he was now in, and was trying to make up for it somehow. This is probably as close to heaven as anyone alive could ever get, Marcus pondered.

As the gravel road kicked up around the back end of the car, they slowly turned a corner and started the upward climb towards the Kananaskis Resort where Marcus would be staying for the next while. Once they reached the top of the long and winding roadway, Marcus could see an isolated lodge resting among the rich, multi-faceted forest.

The driver pulled the car around to the front doors of the Lodge and slowly brought the car to a stop. The plain-clothed RCMP officer now assigned to Marcus while he was in Canada, instructed him to wait in the car while he went inside and checked him into his room.

As the officer opened his door, a swift breeze swept in from the surrounding mountains and blew across Marcus' face. He took a deep breath in, and was astounded by the freshness of the air. Definitely not like the distinctive smog in New York, Marcus thought sarcastically.

After what seemed like an eternity in the car, the officer finally reappeared and told Marcus to follow him into the lodge. With the first step he took into the doorway, Marcus halted in his tracks. Slowly panning the lobby, his mouth dropped slightly open in awe. Surrounding him were authentic log pilings forming the structure of the lodge, with an enormous stone fireplace standing tall in the middle of the room. The fire was roaring, producing heat all the way to the front doors. Its flickering shades of red and orange danced seductively off the glass tables surrounding the large hearth. Oversized plush couches, lounge chairs and dimly lit table lamps also filled the room, giving this the most inviting and relaxing atmosphere that Marcus had ever experienced.

Marcus and the officer proceeded through the lounge area and down one of the long hallways stretching out from each side of the main lobby. Each guestroom door was made of dark, cherry wood, illuminated by the dull wall sconces rhythmically placed along the hallway corridor.

When they finally reached the very end of the hallway, the officer put his key card into the door on the right, waiting for the green light on the door lock to flash, signalling them to enter the room.

"Hang out here for a minute. I just want to take a quick look in the room first," the officer stated.

Marcus stood in the doorway, allowing the officer to do a second inspection of the room. As the officer flicked on the lights in the room, he began to see the outline of the room, which was to be his new home for the next while. The staircase that led up to the plush bedroom loft, the stone fireplace at the foot of the stairs, the oversized sofa placed comfortably in front of it, and the miniature kitchenette with the small fridge, microwave and coffee maker in the corner.

As hard as it was to be away from his family and friends, at least he would be able to be somewhat comfortable in his new surroundings. Once cued by the officer to enter the room, Marcus dropped his duffel bag in the living room and let his tired body flop down onto the sofa.

After a few moments, Marcus realized that the officer had been trying to get his attention. "Marcus," repeated the officer. "Marcus, because you are now in witness protection, you will need to watch your back at all times. Officers will not be visibly around so as to not raise any suspicions about your identity. Someone will always be in contact with you and not far away in case you need us. As far as the hotel is concerned, you are Chris Taylor, visiting from Connecticut."

"The Falcone family thinks you are dead, Marcus. Your family and friends think you are dead. I know this will be hard for you, but we really need you to be strong until the FBI can secure their case against the families. With the help of the Canadian authorities, too, it shouldn't be too long. You're the star witness – hang in there and try to get some rest." The officer left the room, closing the door tightly behind him.

Left all alone with only his thoughts, Marcus got up and turned on the gas fireplace at the foot of the stairs. He walked over to the large patio doors and drew back the drapes. The early fall snow was beginning to drift down. A common weather pattern in the mountains, the light dusting of snow began to accumulate over top of the shrivelling leaves lying on the ground below his window. Marcus gazed up at the luminous mountain ranges engulfing the resort. As the sun tried to set behind the passing clouds, Marcus focused his attention on the streams of light that shone onto the sides of the mountain in front of him.

God, give me the strength to get through this, he thought.

CHAPTER EIGHT

Tony Falcone – infamous leader of the notorious Falcone 'family' based in New York City. His ruthlessness was well known on the streets and the iron-fist he governed the family with was never challenged. Tony was the son of a leading Mafioso member that was born and raised in Calabria, Italy. Tony's father, Nico, had spent his younger years making his way up the chain of command in the Italian mafia. It wasn't until the day that one of Nico's guys turned snitch that Nico packed up his wife and children and moved them to New York City. Once there, he was determined to be an aggressive presence on the city's drug scene. They had arrived at an opportune time – drugs were just beginning to arrive in larger quantities into the city and the competition to disperse them was scarce. Nico immediately put his oldest son, Tony, to work.

The next ten years in New York City proved to be challenging for the Falcone family. The emergence of rival drug gangs and pushers on the city streets was becoming more predominant. In fact, a former member of the mafia family from Italy arrived in the city shortly after Nico, threatening to start their own crime 'family' locally. The Manendo family had arrived in New York City and made their presence known. Lou Manendo, a former friend and confidante that Nico had grown up with back home, emerged as a leading drug pusher in the crime-ridden city. It was during the emergence of these two rivalling families on the streets of New York City that the hatred and loathing for each other really began.

The drug wars between them continuously heated up as they fought to rule the streets. And it was on his hospital deathbed, twelve years into their battle that Nico, who was enduring the final stages of battling prostate cancer, gave his last wishes to pass on the business to his oldest son, Tony. He made sure that Tony understood that their family was NOT to lose business to Lou and the Manendos. He had worked too many years for that.

And with his last breath, he motioned slowly to his head, replicating a gun with his finger positions, and whispered, "Take him out". And that was the end. The hit was ordered, and Tony had to take charge and carry it out – out of respect for his father.

—⋯✻⋯—

"I told you, Tony. Chris, Frank and I made sure he was dead! No more Lou Manendo and no more witness." Alex Falcone was emphatically trying to convince his older brother, Tony that they had successfully carried out the hit.

It was now three days after the boys had killed Lou Manendo, execution-style, in the downtown alley. Once they shot Lou, they heard what sounded like a muffled bang behind the dumpster. Running over to that spot, they found Marcus Leoni crouched in hiding. Without a thought, Frank pointed his gun at the back of Marcus' head and pulled the trigger. Frank, Alex and Chris then fled back to their parked SUV and peeled away into the night.

The streets had been quiet for the past few days. After a big takeout like that, the Falcones had to lay low. Today they'd decided to come together in an old abandoned warehouse on the west side to discuss the events that took place.

"With Lou out of the picture, their family is struggling. I heard that Lou's son, Joey, is trying to pick up the business but isn't as organized as Lou was. He can't get his shit together quick enough. It's our time to take him out while he's stressed. We can be in complete control of the NYC business." Alex made a fist, mirroring the violence of his suggestion. "They're in trouble, Tony - now's our time to strike."

The dim lights hummed from up above them, crackling from periodic electrical surges. Tony was sitting on an old crate in the center of the room, his boys standing around him like soldiers.

"You're right. I like it." Tony lit up another cigarette. "Tell the boys that the hit is out. We're taking out Joey."

"This one's for you, Dad," Tony mumbled under his breath.

On the other side of the city, smoke wafted through the dimly lit room as the Manendo family gathered around the large poker table situated in the middle of the spacious storage room. Located in the back of the Cantare Restaurant on 10th St in New York City, this room was known in drug circles as the gathering place for people working with the Manendos. Security was usually tight, but even more so since the night that Lou was taken out.

The Manendos had made the fatal mistake of loosening their security grip when Lou's main man, Frank, had told them that the supplier specifically requested that Lou come to the meeting spot alone that night. Frank insisted that he had trusted the guy and that he would make sure Lou would be safe.

Frank Bernelli had infiltrated the family two years ago through a mutual drug connection and gained the trust of the Manendo family, and ultimately, Lou Manendo – the leader. This mutual friend was a well-known drug pusher from the streets named Vince.

One summer night, Vince brought Frank to meet Lou at a get-together that the Manendos were having at the restaurant. They were discussing the status of the drug market out of Mexico and its impact on local supply and demand. Frank claimed to have a cousin in Tijuana who had a foolproof way of getting the drugs from Mexico over the border and into the U.S. And with his many associations to the crooked border inspectors, he could give the Manendos the amount of drugs that would make them the ultimate suppliers in New York - just what Lou wanted.

Over the next few years, Frank proved himself to be a ruthless and highly reliable member of the Manendo family. After going through the many stages of proving his loyalty to the family, including grand theft, fraud, and cold blooded murder, Frank was initiated into the Manendo clan. He was present when Lou sent the guys out to cruise the streets looking for any rival drug pushers in the alleys, parking garages and dark corridors.

He rode in their cars as they followed these guys home, and then Frank was the man to pump the fatal bullets through their front windows, finalizing their fate and watching them take their final bow with a sudden drop to the floor.

His emotions were always mixed. He feared that the next hit would be ordered on members of his family, the Falcones. But if it was, then that's what he had to do to keep his penetrated place with the Manendos. That was the deal he made with Tony.

Tony had met with Frank and laid out the intricate infiltration plan. In order to get rid of Lou, Tony was willing to secretly sacrifice some of his own guys. Frank was sworn to secrecy as the plan rolled into motion. The only ones aware of Frank's undercover role, other than Tony, were Chris and Alex Falcone – the ones who were with Frank when he shot Lou. As far as the other Falcone members knew, Frank, a former member of the Falcones, had disrespected orders set out by Tony and had taken off before the hit on him could take place. He went into hiding on the streets and word was he had made his way into the Manendo family, working for Lou to get revenge on Tony.

CHAPTER NINE

Frank had always had a fetish for fast cash and the high life. Growing up in New York's Bronx neighbourhood, there had never been a lot of those to go around. Frank spent most of his days hanging out on the street corners with other local high school dropouts, hustling for money. It wasn't long before they were approached by the Falcone family to sell drugs on the street.

And that's how the relationship between the small, feisty kid known as Frank, and the notorious Falcone family first bloomed. Over the years as Frank's childhood friends moved out of the neighbourhood and on with their lives, Frank became increasingly dependent on Tony and the guys for friendship, and more importantly, family.

His own family has broken up when Frank was young, basically leaving him to fend for himself on the streets of the Bronx. Alex and Tony took him under their wings and raised Frank to be the most feared and respected criminal in New York. Without them, he would have been lost.

Loyalty – that's what he pledged to them in return. "You know, Frank, you're gonna go far in this business." Tony used to always tell him. And when Frank would return from breaking the legs of the drug pusher on the street that would try to steal their business, Alex used to pat him on the shoulders and say, "You're the man, Frank", giving him the feeling of approval he always searched for. And when the Senior Falcone, Nico, passed away, it was Frank that Tony turned to. They created the plan to supposedly 'expel' Frank from the family in order to get him to infiltrate the Manendos.

It took a year or so to implement the plan – slowly leaking rumors of Frank stealing from the Falcones and dealing on the side. When Tony and Frank had their final 'rehearsed' confrontation, they made sure it looked good! With Frank racing out of the building and Tony yelling after him that he was a targeted man.

Frank went into hiding for a year after that. He was in a precarious position. He had to constantly watch his back because if he blinked for a second, his life would be snuffed out by enraged Falcone members, who would be sure to make him suffer a series of torture and humiliating acts in front of his former family.

After that year, he slowly began to emerge back onto the streets. "Hey Frank, where you been hiding yourself?" the street dealers would all say when they saw him.

"You must have heard about the fight I had with Tony," he would always respond. "I had to disappear for a while, but now I need to make some money. Can you hook me up with your supplier?"

And that's how it started. Frank, who was still cautious about running into any of the Falcone guys, had to somehow make his way into the Manendo family. He would speak to Tony secretly every week to inform him of the progress he was making. Tony in return, would steer his unaware guys out of Frank's direction on the streets.

After about six months on the streets, working closely with local street dealers, Frank was finally able to attend a meeting with Lou Manendo. The rest, as they say, is history…

And then there were the Manendos, now headed up by Joey. Hell hath no fury like a drug boss scorned. If they found out about Frank's undercover initiatives, they'd make sure he was floating down the Hudson with the bomb that killed him still taped into his mouth.

Though he often wondered why he would put himself in such a position, the answer was simple - money. Once Tony and he were able to eliminate the Manendos, Tony would set him up for life with all the money he could want, and then help him disappear into the Caribbean. He would finally be free.

CHAPTER TEN

As he slowly blinked open one eye, Marcus felt the warmth of the September sun shining its unassuming rays upon his face. After an exhausting trip the day before, he had settled down for the night with the bottle of Pinot Grigio that the officer had left for him, and allowed himself to succumb to the evening beauty of the surrounding mountains. He gradually fell asleep on the couch in front of the roaring fireplace - the wine bottle balancing precariously on the tips of his fingers, now hanging to his side. This morning was going to be the beginning of a whole new stage in life for Marcus.

Reluctantly, he swung his legs over the side of the couch and placed his head in both hands. *What am I going to do today?*

Determined not to be overtaken by despair, he spent the next hour unpacking and settling into his new home.

"I'm going to go to the front desk and see what's around here," he planned out loud.

After finishing his second cup of coffee on the balcony of his room, Marcus pulled on a fleece sweater and running shoes, clothes from the luggage he had been provided with. He closed the door behind him and casually strolled down the long hallway towards the main hotel lobby.

As he rounded the corner, his attention was drawn towards a large group of hikers that had just returned from an outing on one of the local mountains. Their gear in hand, they seemed in a high state of excitement as they loudly compared stories of how they conquered the various plateaus of the mountain. Marcus walked towards the front desk, brushing past the jubilant group.

In a moment though of sheer slow motion, his glance fell upon a hiker that was staring right at him.

Her blond hair tousled up hastily in a loose ponytail, aqua blue eyes sparkling, her thin frame dutifully following her group of friends through the lobby. Their eyes met for what seemed like a prolonged moment of time, and an instant spark ignited.

Marcus glanced over toward the front desk to make sure he was walking in the right direction, and as soon as he looked back for the mysterious girl, she was gone. The group was still making their way through the room, but the woman with the shimmering eyes was nowhere in sight.

Marcus gave his head a slight shake and figured his sighting was no more than just wishful thinking. Even though he had only been on the mountain for just one day, he was already starting to experience feelings of loneliness and isolation.

Marcus continued his walk towards the front desk and after speaking to one of the reservation agents, learned that there were various walking trails around the resort that he could take advantage of. There were also a number of hiking tours provided all year round, as well as local ski hills that were now preparing for the upcoming winter season.

He decided to go outside and see what his surroundings truly consisted of. Marcus walked out the front entrance and inhaled a deep breath of the refreshing mountain air. With briskness in his step, he began to walk into the morning shadows cast down from the hills.

While on his walk, he pondered his new life, reflected on the old one, and gently wiped away the tears that began to well up in his eyes.

CHAPTER ELEVEN

Three weeks had passed and the drug scene on the streets of New York City was relatively quiet. Both families had retreated for the time being - both strategizing and planning their next moves.

The Manendo family, now headed up by Joey Manendo, was working hard to salvage their existing relationships with suppliers. When Lou was killed, sheer panic ran through the drug chains, putting the suppliers on defensive alert. Attention from the police would be high right now, and none of them could risk being seen or associated with the high profile family. So the daily businesses that Joey ran with his guys selling on the streets had come to almost a complete halt.

Paranoia was starting to set in with everyone, tempers were now flaring, and conspicuous accusations were running rampant over Lou's execution-style slaying. It was obvious to Joey and the boys that the hit had been implemented by Tony Falcone. *But was there anyone else behind it? Anything else he could be missing?* Joey couldn't stop obsessing about the hit that ultimately took his father's life. His dad had been everything to him. As he tried to mourn his death, he started to become overwhelmed with trying to fend off intrusive dealers, keeping the family business on track and fighting the inner rage that now consumed him. Could he still prove his worth to his guys, both in his family and on the street, he often wondered? He had to. One sign of weakness and his life would be taken next.

And it was with those nagging insecurities that Joey pushed forward in the following weeks to make his mark on the streets of New York City. He had to prove that he was completely in control and still able to go head-to-head against Falcone. Still unaware that the deal that had taken the life of the Manendo leader had actually been set up by Frank, Joey continued to make use of his confidante, Frank, and all of Frank's supplier connections – he had no other choice at this point.

"Frank, you need to call your guy in Mexico and confirm the next shipment. We need to make sure that it's still coming in on October 4 and is ready to go. I've got guys waiting for their pick-ups. We have to get production rolling again to start bringing in some more cash." Joey instructed.

Frank dutifully flipped open his cell phone and began to dial. "No problem. I'll get a hold of my guy today and confirm the details."

After an intense two hours on the phone with his supplier, Frank finally met back up with Joey to give him the final instructions for the drug exchange from Mexico.

"You and I are going to meet my supplier down at the Hudson River Docks. This is going to be our biggest shipment so far, so you and I need to be there to make sure that everything gets taken care of when it arrives. We'll bring the boys as backup and place them around the terminal for protection."

The two men, now walking briskly down the alley off 10th toward the back of the restaurant, were on their way to meet with the rest of the Manendo boys.

Frank continued. "The shipment should be arriving around 10:00 AM – just when all the other food market importers will be busy unloading their cargo."

"And the guy from the grocery store in Manhattan – is he set up as the cover?" Joey asked.

Frank gave a slight smirk as he nodded and told Joey, "Absolutely, Joe. He's already been paid and we'll use his incoming shipment for the grocery store as our cover. It's all set. With all the chaos of the morning shipments down there, we should completely get through business unnoticed."

⌒⌁⌇✳⌇⌁⌒

The Falcones, too, had also been making plans for their next move – and it was going to be the final one. At the base of one of the downtown New York City high-rises was where the Falcone clan based their operations. The travel agency - with its 'open' lights brightly reflected in the windows of the surrounding businesses - was the well-known hub of Falcone ventures.

Seated in an oversized leather chair, Tony Falcone slowly inhaled on his morning cigarette while balancing his coffee mug on the cushioned arm of the chair. This was the time he took every morning to quietly ponder life and strategically plan upcoming business transactions. It had been a long time coming, but he now had Joey Manendo right where he wanted him, he thought.

The Falcones and Manendos had longstanding reputations as two of New York City's top mafia families. Tony took another deep drag of his cigarette and slowly let the smoke waft out of his mouth and into the quiet meeting room. He started to smirk as he recalled how Alex described the look that was on Lou's face when he realized he was about to be executed by my guys – a look of total panic. Competition can be a real bitch, Tony thought, as he started to chuckle aloud.

"Watch out Joey…your time is quickly coming."

After a few more sips of coffee, he began to get his mind back to business. He recalled the conversation he had had an hour before with Frank. Frank called to tell him that an exchange was set up with Joey Manendo and the supplier from Mexico at the Hudson River Docks on October 4 – next week. At 10am, Joey would be there to meet his largest incoming shipment of drugs to date.

Determined to kick-start the business since Lou's death, Joey was going to make sure he was on hand to oversee the delivery. Joey would have his boys on hand for protection, but if Tony got there early, he could hide his guys around the terminal first.

Tony pondered the way the hit should take place. Tony confidently leaned back in his chair as a slight smile slowly crossed his lips. He knew exactly how he wanted it done.

Let's go old school, he thought. What better way to finally take down the Manendos than with the gang-style shooting of their new leader in front of hundreds of witnesses. A bold and arrogant move - just like the good old days, he comically reflected.

CHAPTER TWELVE

The past few days in Kananaskis had been long ones, but Marcus was starting to get used to his new routine. Although nothing could compare to being in his own home, around his friends and family, and starting the new job at the hospital in Florida, at least he was put in a place that could only be described as obscenely picturesque.

"Another day on the mountain," Marcus mused to himself as he got out of bed. On this bright morning, Marcus decided to go relax in the lobby lounge with his usually cup of coffee.

He casually strolled down the hall and dropped himself onto a large lounge chair placed comfortably in front of the roaring fire in the stone hearth. He then spent the next hour just watching the onslaught of travelers strolling in and out of the lobby.

He was starting to get into his own routine at the lodge. Most days started off with coffee and a newspaper in the lobby, and then outside for his usual hike through the mountain range. There were numerous hiking trails that were offered in the area, and he tried to make a point of trying out each one while he was staying there. He spent most of his days outside, where the calm and serenity offered him the peacefulness he so desperately needed to fend off his growing loneliness.

He was aware of the ongoing presence of undercover security that followed him around, but didn't seem to mind. It was reassuring to have someone around who actually knew his true circumstances.

On this morning, as he drank his coffee in front of the fireplace, he couldn't help overhear a conversation just behind him.

It was a deep-voiced tour guide on his way out of the hotel. "Thank you so much, Paige, for the great service our group had out here this week. They loved it! I'm going to be arranging another tour out here in the next couple of months to bring in a group of skiers. I'll call you to make the arrangements."

"As always, it was my pleasure, Dave. It's always a treat to have your groups stay here with us! The hike we went on last week was so much fun!"

Marcus couldn't help but be drawn to the conversation as soon as they mentioned the group of hikers that were at the hotel a few days ago. That was when he saw that beautiful girl! As he turned in his chair to see who was speaking, his eyes immediately locked with that same blonde beauty from a few days ago! *She works here?* His heart started to race. *But why haven't I seen her around since then?*

As the young beauty met his gaze with a slight smile, she turned away and started to stroll across the lobby. Marcus, not wanting to give up this opportunity to find out more about her, got up and followed her to the quaint restaurant located on the other side of the central hearth.

He slowed his step and watched as she crossed the restaurant floor and pointed to a private table for two nestled in the corner of the room, up against the picturesque framed window. As she took her seat, he watched as she gently brushed away the blond strands of hair that fell across her eyes. She placed a binder down onto the table and began to make notes on the pages. After a few moments of intense concentration, she paused to bring a glass of water to the tip of her lips and glanced over to where Marcus was still standing. Their gaze met yet once again, and Marcus knew that this was his moment to meet this mysterious woman.

Suddenly aware of the fresh scar now on the back of his neck, he quickly flipped up the collar of his golf shirt to cover it so it wouldn't be seen. He slowly walked into the restaurant and paused in front of her table.

Marcus motioned towards the empty chair across from her. "Is this seat taken?"

"I was hoping you'd come over," she replied with a soft laugh. "Please, have a seat. My name is Paige Torelli. You must be Chris Taylor."

Somewhat taken aback, Marcus wondered in that second if he had just put his security into jeopardy. After all, he WAS in witness protection and nobody around there should know his name – real or fictional.

Sensing his apprehension, she quickly said, "Don't worry, I'm the Manager of this resort. I arranged your check-in the other day but didn't get a chance to introduce myself. Besides, you seemed a bit overwhelmed when you walked in," she chuckled.

"I hope you're enjoying your stay with us now?"

Marcus casually sat down, smiling from ear to ear. "I'm definitely getting used to the beautiful view around here. It's nice to finally meet you, Paige."

Over the next two hours, Marcus and Paige talked over numerous cups of coffee. It was as if they had been friends their whole lives.

Paige, the new Manager of the Kananaskis Resort, had moved to Alberta from Toronto, Ontario. It was there that she had grown up in a privileged family who owned a large bakery business located in Woodbridge, an affluent Italian suburb of Toronto. Although she enjoyed her upbringing within this community and had great relationships with her parents and siblings, Paige had always longed for independence. She was anxious to see what kind of life she could provide for herself without the assistance of her family. When she completed her tourism diploma program at Sheridan College, she immediately started a job at an upscale hotel in Toronto's harbourfront district. It wasn't long before Paige was promoted through the ranks of hotel positions, with her vivacious personality, impressive tourism knowledge and intoxicating beauty. After a few years, Paige had made her way into the position of Operations Manager of the hotel and was enjoying her place within the industry. One day, she received a call from the hotel management company offering her the chance of a lifetime at one of their other resorts. The company had just acquired an upscale lodge in the heart of the Rocky Mountains - Kananaskis Village. Since Paige had impressed the hotel owners with her outstanding abilities over the years, they offered her the opportunity to run the operations of the resort when they launched their opening in

June. Being the free spirit that she was, Paige eagerly accepted the position and began her new journey across the country.

As Paige continued to discuss her journey to Alberta, Marcus became suspended on her every word - the way her eyes twinkled at the discussion of her career goals, the slight laugh she would give as she recounted her childhood, and the tears that would well up in her blue eyes at the mention of missing her family.

"Excuse me, Paige. There's a customer at the front desk that needs to speak to you," interrupted the front desk clerk.

Marcus, suddenly aware that there was a hotel employee standing over them at their table, slowly began to rise out of his chair. Paige stood up and gathered her papers from the table.

"Thanks, Tanya. Please tell them I'll be right there."

Paige looked over at Marcus and gave him an apologetic smile. "I'm so sorry to cut this conversation short, Chris. I guess I really should be getting back to work now." "It's been really great getting to know you. I hope to see you around the hotel again during your stay."

"Don't worry about it Paige. I understand that you need to get back to work. It was great finally getting to meet you! I hope that we can finish our coffee sometime," Marcus replied, giving her a hopeful smile.

He watched her stroll towards the front desk. I'll definitely being seeing you again during my stay, he thought to himself. And with that, Marcus strolled confidently outside of the hotel. He sat himself down on an outdoor nearby bench and raised his head towards the sky. Closing his eyes, he basked in the morning glow of the sun – something he did every day, but which felt almost heavenly today.

CHAPTER THIRTEEN

As the alarm clock sounded, Gabe was abruptly awoken out of his deep, disturbing sleep.   It was his usual 5am wake up call. Unfortunately his day was about to begin just as it had every morning for the past few weeks since his brother Marcus was killed.   Barely getting enough sleep at night, Gabe was still consumed with the agony of losing his twin brother to the violence of the New York streets.   If anyone in the family should have been dead, it was Gabe.

Marcus and Gabe were extremely close growing up as kids - playing stickball in the street in front of their house, hanging out with their friends, and competing with each other for the prettiest girls in school. The only difference, though, was that while Marcus had always been really focused on academics and what he wanted for his future, Gabe struggled through the pubescent years, getting deeply involved in drugs and minor crimes. He ran with the wrong crowd in high school and let them lead him down the path of petty crime, dealing drugs and skipping school to get high. God, if Marcus hadn't tried so hard to pull me out of there, I'd never have survived, Gabe thought.

His gaze slowly drifted over to where his wife, Theresa, lay still asleep. Her expecting belly gently cradled in the soft blankets on their bed. Her light brown hair flowing across her pillow - the angelic beauty that he was lucky enough to have married. Now Marcus will never be able to see his first niece or nephew. A tear gently rolled out of the corner of Gabe's eye as he got out of bed and put on his work shirt. Quickly wiping his face with his sleeve, Gabe continued to get ready for work, putting gel in the front of his hair and messing it around. He had to get going. An early morning shipment was coming in on the docks this morning and he needed to be there by 6:00 to unload and transfer the stock to the warehouse.

"Bye, sweetheart, I'm leaving now," Gabe whispered to Theresa as he slowly walked towards the bedroom door.

"Bye, honey. Have a good day. I love you," Theresa replied, still half asleep. Gabe walked to the kitchen, filled up his travel mug with coffee and grabbed his car keys.

As Gabe got into his car, the sun was just starting to sneak up over the horizon. Another beautiful fall day was expected today, and Gabe was ready to handle whatever came his way.

As he slowly pulled out of the driveway, his eyes caught a flicker of the morning sun. He put on his sunglasses and silently drove off into the sunrise.

CHAPTER FOURTEEN

The morning started off just as any other. Boats entered the Hudson Harbour as the sun peaked its way through the tall New York City skyscrapers. Deep sounding horns announced the arrivals of small cargo ships, while hard working New Yorkers bustled busily around the docks, loading and unloading the shipments.

It was exactly 9:42am and Joey and Frank had been sitting in their Chevy Tahoe since 9:25 in the harbor parking lot. They skilfully watched the busy moving crowds around the docks, looking for any signs of undercover cops lurking nearby. Joey's 'boys' were stationed throughout the docks and inside the main terminal building, holding their positions to protect Joey when he went to meet the drug supplier. Little did Joey know that Tony Falcone had also positioned his men around the terminal too – though for a different reason. His guys were in disguise as shipper/receivers who were working on dock 2. Of course, the owner of the cargo ship at dock 2 was a 'friend' of the family, so to speak.

Joey and Frank were going to meet their supplier at dock 3. The expected ship was a smaller cargo-type ship, which typically could carry a variety of cargo - from produce to furniture - whatever the demand at the time called for. It was just the type of ship that could easily get lost amongst all the other larger cargo ships entering the Hudson River on a daily basis. Its size and ability to disembark at virtually any dock along the route, made it unpredictable.

Plastic coffee cups in hand, Joey and Frank systematically stepped out of their vehicle and started to stroll towards dock 3.

As they walked, Joey looked over at Frank. "You're sure he's gonna be here?"

"I told you, Joey, I got the confirmation last night to let me know that they were on the way as scheduled. They should be comin' in any time now."

As they continued to walk, Frank casually glanced back over his shoulder towards the street. In his meeting last night with Tony, they had discussed how the hit on Joey was going to take place. They had secretly met in the basement of a restaurant owned one of Tony's clients, discussing the fate of their ultimate rival. Between serious plotting and fits of gratifying laughter, they sealed the future of the Manendo family. It would take substantial sacrifice on behalf of the Falcone family, securing the ambush on Joey and preparing for the undeniable shootout that would follow. It would be worth it. It had to be a quick-in and a quick-out though. Once Joey hits the ground, surrounded by his own pool of blood, the police would be racing to the scene.

As Frank glanced over his shoulder, he saw the older model black Pontiac Grand Prix that sat behind a row of cars parked on the street. He turned back around and caught a glimpse of the Falcone guys, dressed as shipping/receiving workers, unloading cargo at dock 3. They were set.

The slight smirk that crossed Frank's face at that moment could only be construed as cocky and egomaniacal. He perfected this plan so incredibly, that maybe he should take over the Manendo family, he thought sarcastically. His immense pride and satisfaction aside, his mind wafted briefly to the beach he would be laying on within the next few days. This was too sweet....

It was at that instant, that the impact of walking into Joey snapped Frank back to his current reality. Joey, frozen in his tracks, could only mouth the words, "The witness.... he's alive!" The witness that was there when his father Lou was executed! The witness that could bring down the rival Falcones!

Joey's heart began to race as he tried to process what he was looking at. This couldn't be right, he thought. Tony's guys took out that guy at the murder scene. Or was he? Did he survive?

Joey turned and yelled to Frank. "We need to get him back to the restaurant before Tony finds him!"

Frank just stood there stunned – almost unable to speak. "The…w-witness!" he sputtered.

This couldn't be happening. Suddenly his dream life at the beach was shattered. Had Tony noticed this guy yet? He glanced back just in time to see Tony standing at the side of the Grand Prix pointing in the direction of Gabe. The directions were immediately clear. The hit was now changed to the guy they recognized as Marcus, or thought was Marcus.

As Gabe sat on a crate at the edge of dock 4, leaning forward with his forearms on his legs, water bottle in hand, he had only looked up for a few seconds before he saw the group of men rushing toward him.

CHAPTER FIFTEEN

For Marcus Leoni, this situation was less than ideal. But for his alias, Chris Taylor, he was in love. He had found the most beautiful, sensitive, and intelligent girl that he had ever met. As he put the finishing touches of gel in the front of his hair, Marcus smiled at the thought of finding Paige in the hotel. He grabbed his jacket off the chair and strolled confidently out the door. Today he was going to see if Paige could join him on his walk around Kananaskis. The views were breathtaking and he was anxious to see if Paige would want to spend some more time with him.

As he entered the lobby area, he caught a glimpse of Paige's blond ponytail bouncing in the air as she scurried from one front desk agent to another, assisting in checking in the Japanese tour group that had just arrived at the hotel.

Marcus leaned up against the side of the colossal hearth in the centre of the lobby, and just watched Paige as she worked. Not one to normally let his feelings get too close to the surface, Marcus concluded that the stressful turn that his life had taken, had caused him to become more receptive to his emotions. He gazed at Paige as she moved in virtual slow motion behind the desk. Her blue eyes sparkled as the early morning sun shone through the front windows, her peach-hued skin glowing radiantly as she smiled, and the sound of her laughter floated across the lobby.

Marcus made his way across to the front desk, catching Paige's eye, as he got closer. She motioned him to the end of the desk, and greeted him as warmly as ever.

"Good morning, Chris! I was hoping I'd run into you today. I just wanted to tell you what a great time I had with you yesterday. I couldn't believe how fast the time seemed to fly!"

Marcus just chuckled. "I was looking for you to see if you wanted to help me do some sight-seeing later. I've been here a little while now, but I'm sure there are some hidden treasures in these mountains that I haven't seen yet."

"That sounds like a date, Chris. I should be able to get off work today around 4:30. There's a beautiful spot up on the Nakiska mountain range with a great view of the sunset. Are you interested in hiking up there with me?" she asked Marcus.

Marcus gave her a charming smirk. "I think I'm up for a good hike. Do you live around here or do you want me to grab a cab and pick you up?"

"Actually because this resort is pretty secluded, the staff of the hotel lives in the resort residences that are around the south side of the building, just down the walkway. It should only take me about half an hour to change and freshen up. How about I meet you here in the lobby around 5:00?"

Marcus tapped the desk with his hand. "Perfect! I'll see you then."

Paige smiled, turned around, and gave Marcus a little wave as she walked back towards the front desk agents. Smiling to himself, Marcus decided to go back to his room and sit on his private balcony for a while.

I need to conserve some energy for what could be a very exhausting evening hike, he thought to himself amusingly.

CHAPTER SIXTEEN

When the shots rang out, the frantic pace down at the Hudson docks came to a debilitating halt. As if the world had suddenly changed the speed dial to slow motion. The people that were normally running at a break-neck pace were now slowly flying through the air in a bid to take cover behind the mounds of crates unloaded onto the docks.

With all the dock workers diving for cover, Tony's men broke through the crowd with guns blazing. The bullets soared through the air, cutting into Gabe's slumped over body as he fell from the crate and face-first onto the cement.

There was a split second in which Gabe gazed toward the heavens and thought of his unborn baby. As if in response, God gave him the image of the most beautiful angel he could ever envision. It was to be his daughter - standing by his side with her face framed by gently flowing curls, and the warmest and radiating light shining from beyond her. And with that peace and love encasing him, Gabe slowly closed his eyes and succumbed to his fate.

Police sirens blared, cutting through the unnerving silence that had fallen around the docks once the gunfire had stopped. The scene that was moments before shrouded in chaos had become a still and eerie tribute to the death of a well-liked dockworker. Stunned expressions still masked the faces of those around Gabe as they rushed to his side to breathe life back into his now motionless body. Before anyone had been able to react to the unimaginable horror they had just witnessed, Tony's men were able to run back to their vehicles and flee the scene.

As soon as Frank realized that he was staring at the mirror image of the witness they had killed a month ago, he knew Tony was going to send out the hit immediately. Once he saw the signal from Tony, Frank sensed the rush of the guns as they ran in behind him, leaving their posts at dock 2. Desperate to keep his cover, Frank grabbed Joey by the arm and pulled him in one quick motion into the dock terminal nearby. Once inside, they got swept into the pandemonium that then ensued. Joey knew that the cops would soon be charging to the scene.

Blending into the rushing wave of people that were now pouring out into the main streets, he knew that he needed to get himself and Frank away from there before they became chief suspects in this shooting.

"Frank, get the car! I'll meet you around the back!"

Pissed off at the botched drug exchange, Joey weaved his way through the frantic crowd, avoiding eye contact with the security personnel rushing past him. As Frank ran to the car, he purposely weaved in front of the Pontiac Grand Prix as it started to pull away from the curb, making a gesture to his head to signal to Tony that their target had been shot in the head. Tony nodded with approval and raced off down the street.

Frank sped toward the back alley of the docking terminal where he found Joey standing against a garbage bin, nervously inhaling a cigarette. The two of them escaped the scene before the cops now arriving could identify them.

As usual, this would be another New York City drug hit that would not be traced to Tony Falcone and his thugs. This career criminal would elude justice for now. But little did he know that this chain of events would ultimately lead to his final demise – and that of his rival's family.

—✻—

It was all over the local and national news stations. A hard-working family man from New York gunned down in a hail of bullets in the middle of the morning rush hour down at the Hudson docks.

In the aftermath of the gruesome scene, police and tactical squads had secured the perimeter and corralled potential witnesses into the dock terminal building, hoping to gain some leads on their impending investigation. As one distraught woman rocked back and forth despondently on a metal bench along the terminal wall, a tall handsome man with a slight limp walked towards her. Police badge in hand, he sat next to her on the bench.

"Miss, I know this is really hard for you right now, but I need you to tell me everything you saw today. Any strange or out of place characters on the docks? Was there any commotion preceding the murder of the dock worker?"

With a pained expression of both confusion and deep thought, the witness recounted how the day had started out just as every other day. "After getting my usual morning coffee, I got to work at the newspaper stand around 5:00 am. Around 5:30, the usual group of workers began arriving for their shifts. Most of them would usually wave hello to me on their way to their dock assignments. Gabe was liked by everybody here. He was always smiling, and told anyone who would listen, about his baby that was due. He and Theresa were so excited. I noticed in the last few weeks though, that Gabe become a lot quieter. It was such a shame to hear about the murder of his twin brother. He became quite reserved and not as talkative. I felt really bad for him and his family."

She continued on to describe how Gabe arrived at his usual time that morning and made his way over to his dock to start unloading from the cargo ship. Although this day seemed the same as all the others, there were two guys that came to the newspaper stand that she had never seen before.

Dressed in grungy jeans and t-shirts, they were conversing feverishly in Italian while waiting for their change. Even though she couldn't understand what they were saying, the strained expressions on their faces made her take a second glance at them while they walked away - their heated discussion carrying on throughout the terminal. Other than that, she couldn't recall anything else until the chaos broke out around 9:45 that morning.

"Well, I appreciate you speaking with me. I know that this was really hard for you. The information will definitely come in useful with our investigation." The detective informed her. He slowly limped away through the dock terminal, lost in his own thoughts. Definitely involves the families, he thought. By looking at the victim, they obviously thought it was Marcus. I didn't even realize that Marcus had a twin. We need to stop these guys and get Marcus home with his family where he belongs, he thought. Let's step this investigation up.

CHAPTER SEVENTEEN

The day had gone by quicker than he thought it would. After sitting for an hour or so on his hotel room balcony having coffee, Marcus decided to somewhat organize the mounds of clothes that were now starting to pile up in his small room.

He climbed up the stairway to the bedroom loft and began to pick up the jeans and t-shirts that were strewn about the floor, carrying them over to the dresser that was situated at the end of his bed. His suitcase was still perched on top of the dresser, the remaining clothes he hadn't worn yet still folded neatly within it. He folded some of the worn clothes and placed them on the dresser. As he did that, he noticed the corner of a picture sticking out from under a pair of jeans still lying at the bottom of the suitcase. Although the witness protection program provided most of the clothing and toiletries, he was allowed to bring along a few personal items from his wallet – which he'd still had on him when he was taken to the hospital that critical night.

He gently pulled out the picture and staggered back down onto the end of the bed. The tears just started racing down his face as he stared at the picture of himself with his family, all sitting around his parents backyard during last year's 4th of July barbeque.

Marcus, his dad and Gabe were all sitting in their camping chairs around the fire pit, reaching their beers up into the air, saluting the holiday. The girls, as always, were seen huddled together on the other side of the fire, laughing at how ridiculous the guys sounded once they started drinking.

This was their traditional family barbeque that they had each year, and everyone made sure that they were there for it. The men would laughingly fight over who could make the biggest fire in the pit, while his sisters would help his mom to marinate the steaks and prepare the feast of pastas and salads. Dad would always put on that stupid barbequing apron that he got when he visited Italy a few years ago – the one with the overweight Italian chef, moustache stretching from ear to ear, juggling a couple of pizzas in the air, Marcus recalled with a smile.

Marcus continued to stare at the picture for a few more moments before lying on his back on the bed, painful tears soaking the blankets on either side of him. This was the first time since everything had happened that Marcus allowed himself to outwardly feel the pain of missing his family – his old life. *I miss them so much,* Marcus thought miserably. *The only positive thing that has happened to me in all of this is meeting Paige,* he reflected.

Marcus got up and walked over to the railing that overlooked the living room down below. With his hands holding firmly onto the rail, he watched the flames flickering in the fireplace below and thought about the past few days getting to know Paige. *I've already had everything important to me taken away, so there is no way I'm going to let someone like Paige slip out of my life,* he vowed to himself. He reached behind his neck and ran his fingers along the inch long scar that was still healing. *I just wish I could explain everything to Paige,* he thought forlornly. *One day I hope.* Marcus wiped away the tear streaks from his face, and turned back towards his suitcase. *What should I wear tonight?*

—ᴄᴏ·ᴄᴀ✲ᴀ·ᴏᴀ—

Paige gazed anxiously at her watch, hoping desperately that her shift was almost over for the day. With only ten minutes left, she started to become extremely anxious to see Chris that night. She frantically rushed through the end-of-day reports on her desk, making sure that everything was in order for the night shift to begin. "Any special plans on this warm Friday night, Paige?" asked one the front desk clerks, fastening her nametag, as she was about to begin her shift. *"Hopefully,"* Paige grinned.

"If my night goes as I'm planning, it should be one to remember."

Paige swiftly took the sweater off the back of her chair and put it around her shoulders. Grabbing her purse, she headed out the front door of the hotel, waving goodnight to the staff as she past. Paige stepped out into the evening air and held her breath for a moment. She was excited and nervous all at once. She softly bit her bottom lip and walked briskly towards her room at the staff residence building, smiling all the way.

CHAPTER EIGHTEEN

"What the hell was that?" Joey yelled at Frank. Sitting in the storage area in the back of the Cantare Restaurant, Joey was still in shock from the events that took place at the docks the day before. He was starting to seethe with anger at the thought that he might have been set up. Up until this week, both families had laid low.

Frank looked completely stunned. "Honestly, man, I have no idea! And did you see the guy they took out at the dock? Looked just like the witness that was there when Lou was hit!"

Frank got out of his chair and started to pace the floor in front of Joey. The rest of the boys were all sitting around a nearby poker table, having been summoned to this emergency meeting. Joey sat on the edge of his chair and lit up another cigarette. As he inhaled deeply, he stared accusingly at Frank.

"And why were Tony's guys there? They must have been tipped off about your boy bringing in the shipment. Coincidence, Frank? Looks like things around here may not be as laid out as I thought they were."

Frank stopped pacing and quickly turned to look at Joey. "I don't know what to say, Joe! I had no idea that they were gonna be there. My contact assured me that this exchange was completely under the radar – just between him and you. I have no idea how Tony's guys found out about it, or where the witness came from."

As the words were coming out of his mouth though, Frank couldn't stop the whirlwind of thoughts spiralling through his mind at the same time. The sudden events that unfolded that day at the dock had completely taken Frank by surprise. Now everything he had worked for would undoubtedly take a drastic turn. Instead of the hit on Joey, the hit would probably be put out on him. It was time for Frank to go to his backup plan.

Frank continued to assure Joey that he had no hand in what took place that day. "Let me make some calls, Joe, and find out what the hell went on."

As Frank stepped outside into the brisk fall air, he knew what he had to do. He quickly walked down the street out of earshot from the restaurant. He pulled his phone out of his front coat pocket and dialed the number he knew would save him. As the phone rang on the other end, Frank's pace began to quicken even more so, while he kept looking back over his shoulder to make sure he wasn't being watched.

The ringing ended with a deep, booming voice on the other end, "Detective Spinosa speaking."

⎯⎯⎯⎯⎯⎯∗⎯⎯⎯⎯⎯⎯

During this time, the Falcones were still reeling at the sighting of the witness they thought they had already killed. Tony called his guys together for an emergency meeting at the travel agency to find out what went wrong.

As the family convened early the next morning, the accusations started swirling around them. The chaos was broken by the thundering voice of Tony yelling at his guys.

"That son-of-a-bitch witness was supposed to be dead!"

The rest of the guys just sat there stunned, as if too afraid to be the one to speak first. After what seemed like an eternity of silence, Alex Falcone spoke up to his brother.

"Man, I told you we took him out after we hit Lou. That guy couldn't have survived that shot to his head. I even went to the funeral myself and watched his family bury him!" he pleaded.

Alex, the second oldest after Tony Falcone, was known as the quieter, more reserved brother. Rarely did he risk standing up to his brother, but in a moment like this, it was necessary to protect his ass and defend him and the team of guys that executed the original hit. He knew that even though he was family, a screw up of that magnitude could have even him 'disappear'.

Tony, absolutely infuriated, continued his tirade. "Obviously you screwed up, Alex! You're just lucky that we found him at the docks and took him out. You guys had better hope that he didn't talk to anyone about what he saw – or heads are gonna roll!"

Tony's words echoed throughout the room. He sat down in his oversized leather chair and leaned back thoughtfully as everyone watched silently. After a moment of quiet deliberation, he finally uttered the command that didn't seem to surprise the guys.

"Find out what happened after we shot the witness - see if Joey or Frank had anything to do with him being kept alive."

In his mind, he was starting to believe that maybe Frank was starting to turn on him and actually working with Joey. Joey isn't smart enough to get his hands on this witness and keep him alive without me knowing, he thought. He had to have help. We need to think about taking out Frank, he decided.

CHAPTER NINETEEN

Putting on a last touch of lip-gloss, Paige took one last look at in the mirror and nodded with approval. Her hair up high in a ponytail, white sweater with brown fleece vest over top, beige khaki pants and running shoes, she was ready for her hike with Marcus. Actually, she told him it was a hike, but she had planned to take him over to the gondola that ran along the side of the Nakiska ski hill, to a beautiful observation point at the top of the mountain. She chuckled to herself, wondering if the 'city boy' was getting nervous about his hike! She locked the door behind her and began to jog over to the front entrance of the hotel. As she opened the front door, she noticed Marcus' tall, handsome frame right away. He stood casually beside the center hearth, his dark blue and white stripped Rugby shirt and jeans gave him a ruggedly attractive look.

Welcoming her with a warm smile, Marcus held out his hand to her as she walked up to him. He laughed as he spoke. "Well…are we ready to tackle a mountain?"

Paige, put her hand comfortably in his, and returned the smile. "Absolutely! You're going to love what I've planned."

Marcus put on his jacket and the two of them then walked hand-in-hand towards to hotel entrance and out to the walkway leading towards Nakiska.

As they walked along the gravel pathway, Marcus and Paige talked as if they had been friends forever. They were so comfortable with each other.

Paige pointed across the mountain, "Chris, if you look over toward the west side of the mountain, you'll notice there's a large rock that extends out beyond the side. Do you see it? It's kind of curved and balanced on a protrusion in the rock."

Marcus squinted, trying to make out the figure that she was referring to. He could see the larger rock on the mountainside, but not much else. "Sort of...what about it?"

"Well, there's a well-known story out here about it. The local aboriginal tribes believe that it's the silhouette of a woman. Legend has it that centuries ago, there was a couple in their late teens that fell madly in love. Their parents, of course, dared not condone the relationship because they were of different tribes. They had happened to meet only by chance one day when the young girl was out hiking on Nakiska, and the young man was sent up that same mountain to look for any rival tribal activity in the area. They met on their journey and instantly connected. For weeks to come, the two lovers secretly met on the mountain top, away from their elders and tribal members. Their love blossomed into a passionate relationship. They even made plans to flee from the reservation and go to British Columbia coastal area in a bid to start a new life together."

Marcus leaned forward. "Really? That's interesting. So what happened?"

"Well, on the day they were going to make their great escape war broke out between the tribes. The young man was sent to war, while the young woman sat anxiously at home waiting for the feud to end. When word came that her tribe had just slaughtered half of the opposing tribe, she raced frantically out to the fields to see if her true love had survived. When she reached the edge of the battle ground, she stopped and scanned the field of bodies. She finally caught sight of him slumped over a large rock and raced over to him."

"Did he survive?"

Paige paused, taking a deep breath before finishing the story. "She ran to him. He was barely breathing. He'd been stabbed in the chest. Crying, she bent down to assist him and heard him whispering something to her. He asked her to continue to their meeting spot and that he would come for her – either in life or in the afterlife. So she kissed him on the mouth, turned and raced up Nakiska Mountain—to the ledge at the top where they always met. He, of course, died on the field, but the young girl desperately believed he would still come for her, so she waited in that spot for the rest of her natural life. She believed his spirit would come down from the heavens and take her to him."

"So you see Marcus, that figure on the mountain ledge is said to be that of the young girl still waiting for her true love."

"What do you think?" Paige asked.

Still strolling hand-in-hand with Paige, Marcus turned to her and smiled. "I think we should make our way up to that spot and see why it was so special for them."

Paige giggled as she looked into Marcus' eyes. "I'm glad you said that! I've arranged for us to take the gondola at the base of the mountain up to that very spot. There's a great sunset observation point up there."

Marcus let go of Paige's hand. "Great! I'll race you to the gondola!"

With that, Marcus started to sprint down the path towards Nakiska, with Paige close on his heels.

"You're on!" she yelled, doing her best to keep pace.

When they reached the spot to get on the gondola, Marcus and Paige were out of breath. A few other couples were already in line waiting for their turn to ride the car up the mountain. Looking somewhat silly being the only people panting and sweating, the pair started to laugh as they got in line.

Marcus had never experienced such an incredible ride. Getting on the gondola was an experience in itself. The enclosed cars continuously moved through the terminal, never stopping. Just before it reached the pick-up spot at the head of the queue, an attendant would open the door and riders were expected to run alongside and jump in the moving car.

Paige hopped in—no problem—but had to pick up an uncoordinated Marcus who literally fell into the car. The two laughed as they sat together on the same side of the car as a second attendant closed the door.

Marcus remarked about the strange feeling he had due to the near vertical ascension of the mountain and marvelled at how close to the mountain's natural wildlife they were. They watched as mountain goats jumped from rock to rock, and the birds flew around and under the gondola as they moved over the trees. Needling him a bit about his awkward boarding, Paige prepared Marcus with a few tips on how to disembark without falling flat on his face. The jump off point was quickly approaching.

Marcus managed just fine and Paige grabbed his hand, guiding him towards the observation deck to the west of the terminal.

Marcus' eyes widened as they walked. "I would never have imagined myself walking along a narrow wooden walkway along the top of a mountain!"

Paige grinned, remembering the first time she had made the trip. "It's pretty incredible, isn't it? If you look down on this side of the mountain, you can see our resort – right beside the golf course."

"You know, Paige, I'm going to have to take your word for it. I don't think I want to look down at this point!" Marcus laughed nervously as he grasped the handrails on the sides of the walkway.

Paige snickered a bit. "No problem, Chris!"

They approached a large open area that looked like a large patio with benches all around. Paige squeezed Marcus' hand and led him to one spot, just above the legendary rock. At her prompting, they sat down on a bench. "This is where they'd rendezvous. They'd sit here and watch the sunset over the Kananaskis valley."

"It's beautiful," Marcus remarked, enthralled with the view of Paige's profile as much as the valley below.

She could feel the weight of his gaze, and turned to face him. They gazed into one another's eyes, relishing the moment, until Marcus leaned over and gently kissed her. As their lips met, they experienced the energy and explosive passion that the two legendary lovers must have felt at that spot. It was magical.

Paige instinctively reached her hand up to cradle the side of his face, and then slowly moved it around to the back of his neck. Completely caught up in the moment, Marcus forgot all about the scar he had been desperately trying to hide. All of a sudden, Paige pulled back and looked around the back of Marcus' neck, seeing the inch long, still freshly healing scar. "What's this?"

Still in shock, Marcus quickly reached up and pulled her hand away from his neck.

"What's wrong, Chris? Why haven't I seen this before?"

Marcus' eyes took on a distant aspect. "It's something that happened in my past that I'm trying to forget about."

He leaned back and attempted to address the concern in her eyes. "It's not important now. Just being here with you is all that's important."

Before Paige had a chance to ask more questions, he re-engaged her with a passionate kiss.

Sensing his unease regarding the scar, she returned the kiss, figuring he would tell her about it when he was ready.

CHAPTER TWENTY

Marcus Leoni, a.k.a. Chris Taylor, was definitely in love. After the date he had just had on the mountain with Paige, he became completely consumed with seeing her as often as he could. It pained him that he had to lie to her about his identity, but he felt confident that one day he would be able to tell her the truth and they could truly be together. For now, he was just soaking in every moment with her that he could.

Paige found herself completely taken with the handsome Chris Taylor. She had never imagined that she would find a man like him in her lifetime. She looked forward to their lunch dates each day and would find herself captivated with his every word. It was definitely love.

Each day, Marcus and Paige would routinely meet for lunch in the hotel restaurant where they first met. And often after her shifts were done for the day, the two would take long strolls along the mountain ridges, taking in the sites and getting to know each more intimately.

During one of their lunch dates, Marcus proposed another date. "So I'm thinking maybe we should go to Banff for dinner tonight? I heard that there's a great restaurant with a mountain view from each table. What do you say, Paige? Are you up for a great dinner, interesting view, classic wine, and ravishing conversation?"

"I don't know, Chris…that would be an awful lot to take in all at once," she teased, giving him her best flirty smile. "Of course - I'd love to. How about we meet here in the lobby tonight around seven? I'll borrow a car from one of my colleagues and pick you up!"

Marcus smiled back. "Great! It's a date."

They continued to finish with their lunch and Paige then reluctantly returned back to work at the front desk, always hating to leave Chris after their lunch dates. Marcus headed back to his hotel room to get himself ready. They both smiled simultaneously, excited to be going out with each other that evening.

What they couldn't foresee was that it was also going to be a night that would provide the most pivotal moment in their relationship – one that would change their lives forever.

⸻✳⸻

The night couldn't have started out any more perfectly. When Marcus came out of the corridor and into the main lobby, he saw Paige standing by the hearth, wearing a classic short black skirt, paired with a gold sequin sleeveless top and black high-heeled sling-back shoes. Her svelte figure was flattered perfectly by the outfit she chose for the date that night. The late-setting sun was sending streams of rays through the front doors, highlighting the flecks of gold in her hair. Marcus smiled and started to walk towards the giant fireplace where she was standing. When he reached her, he gently took her hand in his.

"Paige, you look absolutely beautiful! I'm so glad you agreed to come out with me tonight."

"You're looking pretty handsome yourself, Mr. Taylor." She teased, giving him her most radiant smile.

Hand in hand, the two proceeded towards the front doors and outside into the sunset. The undercover police officers that continued to follow Marcus throughout his daily activities slipped out behind them.

The drive to Banff was a spectacular one. Reminding Marcus of the drive he had taken to Kananaskis initially, this one had the same astounding mountain views, but without the inner feelings of despair. Sitting beside Paige as she drove, Marcus marvelled at the enormous landscape that surrounded them. Seeming so miniscule amongst the giants was a very intriguing feeling. Paige and Marcus talked the entire way to Banff, as Paige relayed the history of the area, as well as pointing out various geographic landmarks along the way. Although Banff was very modern in its variety of shops and upscale restaurants, the architectural designs of the stores and hotels reflecting those that could be found in the Swiss Alps. High, pointed peaks on roof tops, shops placed close together, and store fronts outlined with numerous wood-carved frames gave this town a remarkable European feel.

"Well, what do you think?" Paige asked Marcus as she pulled the car to the side of the street in front of a parking meter.

Marcus leaned forward and peered out the front window.

"It's definitely not something I could have ever pictured. It feels like we're in a completely different country!"

Marcus and Paige got out of the car and walked toward the parking meter, where Marcus insisted on putting in the change needed for the evening. Reaching over towards Marcus, Paige gently took his hand in hers as they smiled at each other and started to walk up the street towards the quaint restaurant at the end of the block.

Keeping with the town ambiance, the restaurant sign hung on a steel rod just above the sidewalk, with a beautifully wood-carved picture of a grizzly bear and the name, 'The Grizzly Cave Restaurant' printed below it. The outside of this restaurant resembled that of a Swiss Chalet, creating a warm and inviting feel for its visitors. Paige pulled Marcus towards the entrance and they walked in.

The restaurant very busy that night. Following the restaurant hostess, Paige and Marcus were seated at a table for two, between the restaurant bar and a large wall of windows.

Marcus ordered from the server. "A bottle of white house wine, please."

Completely engaged in their conversation, the two of them barely noticed when the wine finally came to table. After the waiter poured the wine into their glasses, Marcus raised his for a toast.

"Let's toast to the unforeseen meeting of two great people!"

Paige raised her glass and touched it to his, laughing at his comment.

"I couldn't have said it better myself! What are the odds that two people from such different backgrounds would end up finding each other in a remote village like Kananaskis? I guess it was meant to be, Chris! Cheers!"

Marcus couldn't help but cringe each time she used his alias. He really liked Paige and hated starting off their relationship with such an incredible lie. One day I hope I'll be able to tell her the truth and we can move on, he thought.

It wasn't long before the two of them were eating their main courses, lost in deep conversation. The sun had now set, so the mountain-view was replaced with sheer darkness. Only the glow of the lit candles on each table, and the dim glare from the flat screen TV behind the bar surrounded them. Although the TV had been on since they had arrived, the sounds of the busy restaurant made it barely audible.

The restaurant had now settled into a peaceful quietness. Most of the patrons had moved on to the bars that were lined up along the main street.   As the two of them continued sipping their after-dinner coffees, Marcus suddenly became aware of the TV behind him. The booming voice of the newscaster on the screen made Marcus turn around in his chair to take a look at what was going on.

"Breaking news! The Hudson River Harbour Docks were put on lockdown by the NYPD and FBI earlier today, while they investigated a shooting death of one of the dock workers. In a brazen daylight attack, the worker was gunned down by a group of men who had suddenly rushed at him while he was taking a break from unloading cargo. The FBI is not confirming, but sources at the scene say it looked like a mafia-style hit. The name of the victim has just been released." The announcer fingered his earpiece. "The victim was well-liked dock worker, Gabe Leoni. The motive for the shooting is unclear at this time."

As if the wind had been knocked from his chest, Marcus stumbled out of his chair and staggered towards the bar, keeping his eyes locked on the picture of his brother now posted on the TV screen.

Paige got up and instantly ran over towards Marcus.

"Chris, what's wrong?! Chris? Chris?"

After what seemed like an eternity of staring at the screen, Marcus slowly turned around and locked eyes with Paige, who was now frantic with worry. The tears streaming from his eyes told her immediately that something alarming had just happened.

"I…I…I'm so sorry Paige. I…need to go home."

Marcus grabbed his jacket from the back of his chair and rushed towards the front door of the restaurant. Paige and the undercover policemen were not far behind.

CHAPTER TWENTY-ONE

Still not quite understanding what was going on, Paige sprinted after Marcus, following him to the car. When she caught up to him beside the passenger door, she put her hands on his shoulders and turned him around to look at her.

"Chris, what is going on? What happened back there and where are you going?"

Marcus just stared back at Paige, still reeling from the news he had just heard.

"Paige, I'm so sorry."

Suddenly the tears started streaming down his cheeks. Completely unfazed by the evening traffic still cruising past them, he took Paige's hands in his.

"My name isn't Chris Taylor. I'm not out here on vacation. My real name is Marcus Leoni and I'm from New York City. I'm an emergency room physician who was supposed to be practicing in Florida right now," he hurriedly explained.

"About a month ago, I witnessed the execution of a major mafia boss by a rival family. They saw me and came after me, shooting me in the back of my head. The doctors saved me in the hospital, but the FBI immediately put me into a witness protection program. They think I'm dead, Paige. My family thinks I'm dead. I'm out here waiting for the D.A. to get their case together against the drug families so that I can then go back to New York and testify against them."

As the snow started to gently fall around then, Paige gently put her arms around Marcus' shoulders and pulled him close to her for an embrace. She could feel his body shaking as he started to quietly sob into her shoulder.

"That was my twin brother that was murdered at the docks, Paige. They must have thought he was me. I have to get back to New York City. Please drive me to the airport."

Marcus was desperate. He needed to get back to his family.

As the two of them started to get into the car, Marcus was approached by the undercover agents that had followed them out of the restaurant.

"Marcus, you can't just leave Witness Protection! These guys will kill you the moment you step back into New York City." The agent advised him.

"We can't force you to stay, but you're the only surviving witness that the FBI can use to put these guys in jail! Seriously think about what you're doing. You're going to put yourself AND the investigation at complete risk."

Marcus continued to climb into the passenger seat of the car.

"I'm sorry, but I'm done here. I have to go home."

Leaving the agents helpless as they stood idle on the side of the street, Paige put the car into gear and headed towards the TransCanada Highway – bound for the Calgary International Airport.

On the drive out of Banff, Paige just stared straight ahead in amazement – having difficulty dealing with what Chris, or rather, Marcus had just told her. The life she thought they had been living up until now was a complete lie. Feeling both betrayed by the lies and sympathetic to Marcus' situation, she began to cry. The drive to the airport became an emotional blur as they both sat in silence. Paige continued to drive, tears streaming down her cheeks, while Marcus stared out the window, now seething with rage over the murder of his brother.

Just before reaching Calgary's city limits, Paige suddenly looked over at Marcus. Sobbing, "Marcus, this is crazy! You're going to get killed if you go back."

"I have to, Paige. You can't understand what they've taken from me. I've had enough and it's time to take things into my own hands."

"What are you saying, Marcus? You're going to go after them? That's suicide!"

"I'm sorry. This is something I have to do."

Marcus turned and continued to look out the window. The mountains were now a distant memory, almost completely out of view as they entered the city of Calgary. He had to focus and come up with a plan – his life depended on it.

CHAPTER TWENTY-TWO

Travelers rushed around in a flurry of activity as they made their way to their destinations. Children dragged their small character suitcases behind them, with their favorite stuffed animal tucked under one arm and soft security blanket under the other. Impeccably groomed business men and women hurriedly paced through the terminal, speaking emphatically into the cell phones attached to their ears. And although this type of madness would have increased a level of excitement in most people there, Marcus was consumed with a desire for revenge as he sat in the coffee shop at the Calgary International Airport.

Seemingly unfazed by the rush of travelers around him, Marcus stared furiously into his coffee cup, swirling around its contents while planning his wrathful vengeance. The pain and rage that he felt at the moment could not even be described with words.

His twin, Gabe, was not only his brother. They seemed to share a soul. Like most twins, Gabe and Marcus had an unspeakable bond that allowed them to feel what the other felt, say what the other was thinking, and above all, love each other as if they were each one half of the same person. Gabe's murder shook Marcus to the core. He was hell-bent on revenge. It was bad enough that those arrogant families could try to take away his life and future, but to go after Gabe! *What has our family ever done to deserve this? Nothing. There is no way I'm going to let them get away with ruining my life and that of those around me.*

"…United Airlines Flight 949 departing for New York City is now boarding at Gate D", the ticket agent announced over the loud speaker.

As Marcus stood up and looked at his plane ticket, the assumed name of Chris Taylor seemed to taunt him, to compel him. The desire to take control of his life swept over him. It was time to reclaim his true identity and retaliate for the pain caused to his family. Marcus clenched his fist with determination as he pictured Gabe's baby growing up without a father. *This one's for you, Gabe!*

As he walked assertively to the gate and boarded, the mundane details of the world around him faded into the background. A steely focus seemed to guide his every move.

CHAPTER TWENTY-THREE

As Marcus got off the plane at JFK International Airport, the usual hustle and bustle of the weekday New York travelers swirled endlessly around him.   He stood amongst the growing crowd of travelers waiting for their luggage to come bouncing down the carousel.

After finally grabbing his bag, Marcus made his way towards the airport exit. Stepping out of the airport doors, the electric sounds of the city he once called home, welcomed him in an unexpected way. Still feeling apprehensive about being spotted by one of the crime families, he also felt somewhat reassured and at ease by being in the city so familiar.

Marcus held out his hand. "Taxi!"

As usual, the endless sea of yellow cabs racing through the terminal made it hard to nail down a single one. Finally, one stopped for Marcus and he jumped in.

"Holiday Inn Express Manhattan...on 5th, please," he instructed the driver.

The cab driver glanced back over his shoulder at Marcus.

"No problem. So where are you from?"

Marcus sat back in the seat and let out a deep breath.

"Actually, I'm not sure lately."

After a few seconds he continued, "I grew up here in New York."

"What brings you back?" the driver asked, somewhat confused.

Marcus turned and stared out the window. "Family."

The rest of the drive through the city was a quiet one. As the cab pulled up in front of the hotel, Marcus stepped out, paid his bill and then grabbed his bags. He walked into the lobby and stood still for a moment. A flashback of standing in the lobby at the Kananaskis Lodge when he first arrived came rushing to mind. He missed seeing Paige working behind the desk at the hotel each day. He missed seeing her blonde ponytail bouncing gently in the air as she approached him at the restaurant for their daily lunch date. He missed her so much.

I have to do this though, he thought. I'll make sure I go back to Nakiska to find her once I can get my family back together. Hopefully she'll still be waiting for me, he thought sadly.

"Can I help you, sir?" the hotel clerk called out to him. With a quick nod back to reality, Marcus proceeded to the desk and checked in.

CHAPTER TWENTY-FOUR

Marcus sat at the work desk in his hotel room, the light reflecting from the desk lamp into his blue eyes. His plan was to lay low - he couldn't risk being detected by the Manendos or the Falcones. Avoiding his family was also going to be hard but necessary in getting this plan executed and securing their safety.

He picked up the desk phone and made his first call - to the secret undercover officer that the FBI had given him the number of. He had to start putting his plan into motion.

After an intense conversation with the local agent, he sat back on his bed, still working out the details of his plan in his head.

It wasn't long before a sudden knock on his hotel room door startled Marcus, who was now completely lost in thought. Feeling extremely apprehensive, he slowly got up and approached the door. Marcus positioned himself to one side of the door and guardedly peered into the peek hole. The person standing on the other side of the door stared back at him, although not actually seeing him.

Marcus was extremely surprised to see this visitor. He hadn't expected for his plan to begin moving so quickly. Recognizing the NYPD badge that the visitor held up, Marcus quietly unlocked the door and opened it wide, ushering in his guest.

The agent stepped into the room, slightly limping, and held out his hand to greet Marcus. "It's nice to finally meet you. I'm Detective Spinosa – we spoke earlier on the phone."

"As I told you during our conversation, I think you've got a plan in mind that could actually work. That's why I'm here – to discuss the details. My RCMP contacts in Canada had given me the heads up that you were on your way back, so I wasn't surprised to get your call. I am surprised, however, that you want to take on these ruthless crime families. They're extremely dangerous."

The agent and Marcus sat down on the couch to continue their conversation.

"You may not know this, but I was the one who found you the night you were shot. I specialize in local gang crime and had followed Lou Manendo that night. I was crouched behind a car just down the alley from where you were, and I also saw the Falcones execute him. When Lou fell to the ground, you had inadvertently banged your foot against the garbage bin – no doubt jumping from surprise at the sound of the gunshot. I saw Alex Falcone point in your direction and they rushed behind the bin to where you were squatting. One of the guys kicked you in the head, which caused you to fall over on your stomach, and then Alex pointed the gun to the back of your head and fired."

The detective dropped his gaze and slowly shook his head.

"I'm so sorry, Marcus. There was nothing I could do to save you until they ran off. Once they did, I ran to my car and drove to where you were laying, put you in the back seat and drove you to the emergency room. I made contact with my police captain and told him what happened. He then arranged for you to be rushed to an isolated area of the hospital when you arrived. While you were recovering, the FBI met with the Canadian RCMP to arrange for your trip to Kananaskis. I couldn't stay around the hospital and risk blowing my undercover status."

Marcus leaned back against the couch.

"Wow. I had no idea all that was going on. I'm just so thankful that you were there for me in the alley. Otherwise, I wouldn't be here."

"Are you sure you want to go through with this, Marcus?"

Marcus looked over at the agent.

"You know, detective, I've had a lot of time to think about what these guys have done to change my life. When I arrived in Kananaskis, I felt resigned to just go with the plan laid out for me by the police, getting myself ready to testify against those guys. But when I was there, I met someone who made me realize that a great life is worth fighting for. And then when I heard what they did to Gabe – that just sent me over the edge!"

"I needed to find a way to make sure these guys paid for what they've done to me and my family."

"You know you're not safe, Marcus. They took Gabe for you and look what happened."

"I know. But my twin brother died and I survived. Why is that? You were there to save me, but I wasn't there to save Gabe. I need to step up and at least try to avenge his death."

Marcus took a deep breath before continuing. "They've terrorized my family, who not only thinks I'm dead, but are burying Gabe tomorrow. It's not fair – I need to *do something*. That's why I called you. Can you get the explosives we talked about?"

The detective sat back and crossed his arms in satisfaction.

"I arranged it with my supplier. He'll get them laid out where we discussed. Trust me, Marcus. I've been after these guys for years and wouldn't miss this opportunity to take them off these streets."

The two continued their plans to go head to head with the infamous crime families of New York City.

CHAPTER TWENTY-FIVE

It was as if the heavens were mirroring the pain that Marcus felt. The day of the funeral arrived with dark, luminous clouds streaming steadily across the skies. Marcus would not miss the chance to pay respect to his brother.

He dressed and made his way down to the lobby. After hailing a cab, he made his way to the cemetery – cautious about being watched or followed. From the back seat, Marcus leaned forward and pointed just up the street.

"Drop me off over here."

As the taxi drove away, Marcus gazed up the street – he was now standing three blocks away from the actual cemetery entrance. He knew that the families may be watching the cemetery that day to make sure that Gabe was actually buried, so Marcus had put together somewhat of a disguise for the trip. Pulling his black fedora low over the top of his eyes, he flipped up the collar on his long rain trench coat and walked slowly up the street. Sunglasses on, even though it was still casually raining out, he prayed that he would be able to say goodbye to Gabe from a distance without being recognized.

Marcus made his way onto the cemetery grounds and found a spot behind a group of low hanging willow trees. He had a clear view of the burial plot as well as the funeral procession as it now made its way along the driveway. As the procession stopped, Marcus held his breath as he caught sight of his mother, looking rapidly aged since he last saw her, stepping out of the limousine. Tears streamed steadily down her face as she slowly walked toward the freshly dug burial plot. Being helped by Marcus' dad, and followed by Gabe's expecting wife, the sight became almost too much for Marcus to bear.

This must be how it looked when they thought they were burying me, he thought. He looked away and allowed his pain to release in a raging race of tears.

He set his gaze upon the ceremony now taking place, with the priest offering blessings over Gabe's casket as it was being steadily lowered into the ground. Gabe's wife, inexplicably pained, let out a shrill cry of anguish that resonated throughout the entire cemetery. Birds suddenly rose from out of the surrounding trees, startled by the sudden outpouring of grief. The suffering anguish blanketed the cemetery until the time came for the mourners to say their final goodbyes and return to their existing lives.

Once everyone had left, Marcus slowly and cautiously made his way over to where the head stone had been placed.

Now standing over his brother's final resting place, Marcus stared at the beautiful picture of Gabe and his wife that now leaned against the head stone. Memories of life growing up with his brother came flooding to his mind. Marcus said a little prayer, begging the angels to carry Gabe's wonderful soul on top of their wings and up to the heavens above.

"I'm so sorry, Gabe that you got caught in this. I'll take care of Theresa and your unborn child. I promise." He said under his breath.

"I won't let these guys get away with what they did to our family."

And with that, Marcus turned on his heel and defiantly strode through the cemetery – his mission playing out in his head.

CHAPTER TWENTY-SIX

The plan was in motion. The morning had the cold, crisp breeze that was expected on such a beautiful fall morning in the city. With every step Frank took, sheets of newspaper whirled in the wind around his feet as if trying to hold him back from the mission he was about to embark on.

Abruptly stopping, he ducked into the alley behind the restaurant where the Manendo family routinely converged. With a rhythmic knock on the back door, Frank was let in by one of his family members. Even for being so early in the morning, the room was filled with smoke wafting through the air – obviously it had been a late night that hadn't ended yet.

Frank walked his way through the groups of tables and lounge chairs over to where Joey was sitting with seven of his top guys. Lounging back in his plush leather chair, with a coffee in one hand and a sizzling cigarette in another, Joey gazed up at Frank as he approached.

"Joey, my dealer from the docks has contacted me to arrange for another buy. He went into hiding after the shit that went down at the dock that day and hasn't been able to sell his supply. He's willing to sell you the whole thing. He's got the best cocaine ever produced - enough supply to easily bring in $3 mil on the street. He wants to get rid of it so he can leave the city. He'll sell exclusively to you for $1.4 mil. Basically man, you'd be the main dealer in New York and will double your initial investment."

Frank sat down next to Joey as he continued to propose the new plan.

"This could be the best deal to ever come to us, Joe. You'd then become the supplier's main man when he brings in his shipments each month. You'll be able to drive Falcone out of business and then take him out when he's down."

The room became uncomfortably silent. It seemed like forever before the silence was broken by Joey's forceful voice. He leaned forward in his chair as if to engage Frank in challenging conversation.

"It can't be that easy, Frank. I didn't get in this position by being stupid or naïve. My dad would even have questioned this deal. What about all the shit that happened at the dock that day? Tony and his guys where there...no doubt to take me out. I don't know what happened that day, but I'm not gonna be set up again. And God help the guy that arranged THAT hit."

"Honestly Frank, I don't trust your supplier – or even you for that matter."

Joey sat back in his chair while the surrounding guys just remained respectfully quiet.

Frank, trying to keep absolutely calm and confident, stood up in front of Joey and looked him straight in the eyes.

"I'm telling you, Joey, I don't know how Tony found out about our buy that day. The supplier is freaking out right now, stuck with all his drugs. He's desperate to dump it and get back to Mexico to get his next shipment before his rivals take it. We can use our dealers on the street to secure the perimeter around the buy, as well as have our guys in defensive positions around you. In my opinion, now is your chance to make your final move against Tony. Make yourself a huge profit, and put Tony and his guys in their grave. What more could you ask for? Think about it for a while. You know how to get a hold of me if you decide to take the deal."

Frank confidently turned around and strode toward the back door. Once the door closed behind him, he stopped and looked up toward the rising sun. Taking in a deep breath of crisp morning air, he silently prayed to God that this would work. It had to – his life depended on it.

"…in my opinion, now is your chance to make your final move against Joey," Frank boldly told Tony Falcone.

Now sitting across from Tony Falcone and four of his top 'family' members, Frank repeated the same story to Tony that he had a day before presented to Joey Manendo.

Tony, much like his rival Joey, seemed very skeptical of the deal being put forth in front him. It was his duty as the family leader to make smart decisions that would put his family first and foremost on the drug scene in New York – through reputation, intimidation and wealth. Street smarts were what got him there, and he needed to rely on them once again to make the best decision for his guys.

But maybe Frank had a point though. Maybe now was the time and opportunity to make a pivotal move.

"…so you think about it, Tony. Let me know what you decide. You know how to get hold of me," Frank continued, breaking through Tony's thoughts.

With that, Frank sparked his lighter and inhaled deeply on his cigarette, keeping eye contact with Tony the entire time. He confidently turned and strode out of the room, up the stairs, and into the above restaurant.

Standing at the front of the restaurant, now filled with hungry lunchtime diners, he remained calm and proceeded to walk through to the front door without arousing any inquisitive glares. He continued to walk briskly down the street to his parked SUV.

As he climbed into the front seat, he sighed heavily, reflecting on the weeks' events. The traps were in place. Now let's see if the fish will bite, he thought.

He picked up his cell phone and dialed a number that had recently become very familiar to him. He waited impatiently for his call to be answered. Finally he heard the familiar voice he so desperately needed at this point, answer his call – "What do you got?"

CHAPTER TWENTY-SEVEN

Marcus stared silently into his steaming cup of morning coffee. Sitting in the hotel restaurant had become his new morning routine. So many sleepless nights were now taking their toll. Looking visibly drawn and tired, he wrestled with his emotions on a daily basis – missing his family, mourning Gabe, and feeling heartsick from losing Paige.

It was the sudden ringing of his cell phone lying on the table that now startled Marcus, causing him to spill his coffee. "Hello", he answered with hesitation.

"Marcus. Frank called. Both Tony and Joey took the bait. The plan is going ahead."

Marcus squinted and stared straight ahead. *Finally, we're going to do this –for you Gabe.*

The next few days were a complete flurry of activity for everyone involved in this set up. It was such a risky plan, but could save the lives of many people in the future, and release New York from the grips of these drug families.

Marcus spent most of his time in his hotel suite on the phone with Detective Spinosa. The detective became an integral part of the plan. With his undercover connections, he did most of the leg work and made all the arrangements that needed to be done. The day that was picked to execute the plan was Thursday, November 3. This would be the day that everyone in the plan would come together and play their critical roles. The final call came in to Marcus' cell phone on Monday, October 31 from the detective.

"Marcus, the supplier has delivered the explosives to the warehouse and my guys installed them all around the inside of the building. We'll get Frank to arrange for Tony and Joey to meet their drug supplier there on Thursday at 9:00 and 9:30pm respectively. Neither of those guys will know what hit them."

"Frank is quite confident that Tony and Joey trust him enough to go through with the supposed buy at the warehouse. This is our best shot. Let's make sure it works."

Marcus responded with an unsure tone in his voice.

"I hope so. Otherwise my life isn't ever going be the same."

And I want to make sure that I make it back to meet Paige in Nakiska, he thought optimistically.

CHAPTER TWENTY-EIGHT

The morning of reckoning arrived. Marcus awoke to the sounds of a host of birds chirping their daily cheer, inspiring one another to seize the day.

Well, today was Marcus' day – a day of vindication and future freedom. Although he awoke to the same group of birds every morning, he never really understood their morning ritual until today. Rallying the troops and psyching them up for the day.

Marcus slid himself up in bed and anxiously rubbed his eyes. Getting out of bed, he prepared what he hoped would be his last pot of hotel room coffee.

With the aroma of fresh brewing java filling the room, Marcus packed his duffel bag, pausing as he came across a picture of him and Paige sitting on a large rock in Kananaskis, the sun setting behind the mountains in the background. *I'll come back for you Paige*, he vowed. He placed the picture in the front pocket of the suitcase and continued to pack.

When his coffee was ready, he sat down for the last time at the in-room desk and dialed the number for Detective Spinosa.

"Is everything ready?"

"You bet, Marcus. I've already spoken to Frank this morning, and he's got his instructions for today. Everyone is ready. Are you going to be okay?"

"More than you know. Today, my nightmare will finally end and I can begin my life again. Let's do this. I'll contact you later to confirm everyone is in place."

"Take care, Marcus. Be careful out there. I'll see you at our final meeting spot," the detective instructed.

Marcus hung up the phone, took one last sip of coffee, and grabbed his suitcase. A few minutes later, he was standing in the hotel lobby for the last time. "Will you be checking out today Mr. Taylor?"

"Definitely," Marcus responded with a slight smirk.

CHAPTER TWENTY-NINE

That day had begun with the most peaceful sunrise that New York City had ever seen. As the daily boats floated in and out of the harbour, the tourists started to flock to the streets with their cameras in one hand and morning coffees in the other. Birds soared gracefully above the illuminating high-rise buildings of downtown while office workers systematically made their way to work.

As the day carried on, the peaceful and quiet start to the day began to waiver. It became clear that the morning had become the calm before the storm. Dark, smoky clouds had started to role across the sky, bringing heavy snowflakes with them. Sporadic, large flakes drifted through the streets, carried by the angry winds that had begun to soar through the streets.

Sitting at a corner table in a rundown coffee shop near the Hudson docks, Frank shifted nervously as he prepared to call Tony and confirm the meeting with the supplier that night. If something goes wrong tonight, his life was over – not a doubt. Setting up the two main drug families in New York City, as well as becoming a secret police informant basically signed his death warrant.

Could he have just stayed with the original setup working for Tony to take out Joey? No way, he thought. Not since that witness showed up again and ruined the takeout plan at the docks. No, both families became too suspicious of him at that point.

Frank made his first call.

"It's all set, Tony. The supplier will be at the abandoned warehouse on the corner of 8th and Denver at exactly 9:00 tonight. He said that he'll wait inside because the drugs are on pallets along the back wall. Bring the boys and their trucks to load them up and take out the back door. He said he's got 6 pallets for you and wants you to make sure you bring the $1.2 million that we negotiated him down to. Keep it on the up, man - it's my ass on the line if this goes bad."

"Ok, Frank. But I'm warning YOU. This had better be the real deal or you won't live to see tomorrow. Make sure you're at the back of the building when me and the boys bring the trucks around." Tony replied threateningly.

"You won't regret this Tony. In fact, you may even want to give me a bonus for setting up this deal," Frank chided nervously. "I'll see you and the guys at 9."

As he hung up the phone, he walked outside to light up another cigarette. Standing outside on that crisp, clear morning, Frank prepared himself for the next call he had to make – the one to Joey, relaying the same information. He inhaled a deep, stale breath from his cigarette and started to dial Joey's number on his cell phone.

"....I'll see you and the guys at 9:30. Remember to park at the front of the warehouse, beside the door. Ciao Joey," repeated Frank.

It's all set. Tony and his guys will pull up to the back of the warehouse at 9:00 and then go inside to check out the pallets with the drugs. While they're inside, Joey and the boys will pull up in the front and then go inside. *Once the two groups see each other inside, the sparks will fly*, he thought. *Literally*, he smirked.

CHAPTER THIRTY

Frank stared at his watch, anxiously anticipating the arrival of Tony's car. It was already dark outside and the shadows of the night were already being cast across the parking lot.

As if sensing Frank's anticipation, headlights slowly turned through the dark streets, rounding to the back of the blackened warehouse. The Grand Prix slowly pulled up and stopped in the darkness beside the back door. Two more vans slowly pulled in behind the Grand Prix and parked. Frank made his way to the passenger side of the lead car and opened the door for Tony. Frank stood tall and confident.

"Hey, Tony...the supplier, John, is inside and the pallets are ready to be loaded. Got the money?"

"Of course I do," Tony replied, stepping out of the car and standing face to face with Frank. Coming this close to one of the most powerful men in New York made a chill run down Frank's spine - but for the sake of the plan, he remained stoic and returned the intimidating stare.

"Frank, take us in. You go first. I want to make sure that any traps inside will take you out first," instructed Tony.

The rest of Tony's guys made their way to where Tony and Frank were standing. The air became eerily silent as Frank turned and led the guys to the door and then inside.

This warehouse hadn't been used in years and the dusty, stale aroma reflected that. With only a dim light shining in the back area of the warehouse, Frank led a cautious Tony and his guys to where a middle-aged man in jeans, t-shirt and baseball hat stood waiting in front of six loaded pallets.

The pallets were filled with taped up brown bags, each piled 4' high. Frank stopped in front of the pallets, as Tony slowly walked past him and over to one of the piles.

"Tony, this is my supplier, John."

Tony did not speak a word. Everyone knew the routine at this point and just watched as Tony proceeded to check out the drugs. Keeping his eye on the supplier, Tony aggressively lifted up one of the taped bags. Pulling out the switch blade he always kept tucked into his side pocket, he slowly made a 1" incision into the top of the bag. Scooping a small amount of white powder onto the side of the gleaming blade, he systematically brought it up to his nose and inhaled with one quick sniff. After pausing for a moment, allowing the cocaine to flow throughout his body, Tony gave a slight nod of approval to his main guy. This was the stuff.

John locked his gaze with Tony once again and simply stated, "Now the money."

Tony confidently looked over his shoulder at one of his guys, and gave him the nod to bring up the suitcase. The guy strode up to the pallets and laid the small suitcase on top. John leaned over the packages of cocaine and began to unzip the suitcase.

As he lifted the lid, he could hardly process the amount of $100 bills staring up at him. At the precinct, he would never earn this amount of money in his whole policing career.

"Is it all here?" he asked, picking up a bundle of hundreds and flipping casually through it.

Tony looked at him arrogantly.

"The $1.2 million we agreed on. We got a deal?"

John locked eyes with Tony.

"Sure. I need to move this stuff and get back to Mexico. Back your vans up to the back door and I'll move the pallets over there for you."

John turned and proceeded to walk towards the fork lift, trying hard to conceal his chronic limp.

Within 15 minutes, John had moved the skids to the back door, while Tony supervised his guys loading the sealed packages into the vans. Unknown to him, his number one rival had just arrived at the front of the warehouse, being greeted by Frank, who had casually blended into the darkness of the warehouse once the loading began.

Once out of sight of the Falcone members, Frank had raced his way through the weaving hallways of the defunct warehouse. He stopped himself meters away from the front entrance to wipe off the beads of sweat that were now racing down the side of his face. He had to look casual.

Once composed, he stepped outside into the dimly lit front of the building, and awaited Joey's arrival. It didn't take long before the cavalcade of SUV's rounded the corner, headlights off. As the warehouse was quite large, the low hums from the engines arriving at the front could not be detected around the back where Tony and the boys were still loading up.

Frank greeted Joey as he stepped out of his vehicle.

"Right on time, Joey. Our supplier, John, is waiting inside."

Joey and his boys strode up toward an awaiting Frank, standing just in front of the door.

Joey looked impatient.

"Let's get moving, Frank. I've got other things to do tonight."

Frank turned towards the door and prayed that phase two of the plan was already in place. With the abandoned building being so oversized and the lights dimmed out, it shouldn't be too hard to get Joey's guys into place unnoticed by Tony on the other side, Frank thought.

As Frank led Joey and his men into the building, a guy with jeans, t-shirt and baseball cap was standing off to the side beside six pallets loaded with taped up bags. The same set up had been duplicated for Joey.

Of course neither Joey nor Tony had any idea that the top bags were full of pure cocaine - the remaining bags full of powdered sugar in order to fill up the pallets.

As the same scenario took place with the supplier, John, Frank kept watching the other side of the room to make sure Tony didn't surprise them by walking in.

"…I'll move the pallets to the front door for you to load in your vans. Don't worry about being seen. This street has been abandoned for years and nobody uses this road anymore. You may have noticed that I also shot out the street lights to make it darker for you," stated John as he turned toward an awaiting fork lift, again trying to mask the obviousness of his limp.

As the bags were being loaded into Joey's SUVs, Frank stayed with Joey, making sure they were happy with the load and that things were moving smoothly.

John, who had moved the pallets to the front doors for Joey, raced his way to the back of the building ahead of Frank to check on Tony. When he arrived, Tony was busily talking with his guys who were now about half way through loading the vans.

John approached Tony and was making conversation with him to divert his attention from the back door where Frank was now slipping out of. Once Joey got busy with his guys loading their vans, Frank once again slipped away into the darkness and raced across the warehouse to the back where Tony was.

John was still talking with Tony as Frank walked up.

"..I wasn't going to even mention the guns, but you seem like a straight up guy. I've also got a load of the high-powered AK-47's back in the warehouse. I'll give you a good price for them since you took the coke. Interested in taking a look?" John was asking Tony.

After a moment of silence, Tony nodded his head to his guys and yelled, "Take a break. I want you guys to come back in with me and check out some guns."

Frank couldn't believe how well this was coming together!

"You know, Tony, this night seems to be working out really well for you and the boys. I'll go ahead with John and help him get out the guns from the back room. Keep loading the coke and give us about 10 minutes to get the skids out for you to look through."

Frank turned and started to jog back into the warehouse with John beside him.

Once out of sight, Frank bolted to the front of the warehouse where Joey and his guys were about a quarter of the way through their pallets.

"Hey, Joey! I just talked to John and he said that he's also got a shipment of AK-47's in the warehouse that he needs to get rid of. He wants to know if you're interested in taking a look. He'll give you a deal if you want any."

At that moment, Joey was feeling like the drug wars were now his to own. The drugs were in his possession and he would finally be able to outsell Tony on the streets. With a whole new set of guns and ammo, they could probably even finish Tony and the boys off for good, he thought.

"You know, Frank, you done good today. I'll take a look at the guns while the boys finish loading the vans."

"You should bring the boys in with you, Joey. I'm sure they'll be carrying them right back out for you!" Frank said, trying to sound convincing.

"You're right. Boys, take a break!" Joey yelled, as he turned and followed Frank back inside the building.

CHAPTER THIRTY-ONE

The air was electric. The mixture of arrogance, confidence, and condescension filled the warehouse as the two most infamous drug families in New York City each advanced from opposite ends of the darkened warehouse, into the middle of the building. This was now going to be either the end as Frank new it, or the beginning of the life he now so desperately needed.

"Mother fucker!" was heard echoing throughout the room with a thunderous, enraged sound. This was his chance. Frank, who now balanced the emergence of the two families approaching one another, knew that this was his moment. Once the eye contact was made between Tony and Joey, Frank made no hesitation as he took off in a desperate race for his life, towards the emergency exit at the side of the room. Frank had barely made it to the exit when the explosion of gunfire had erupted. Shots rang out amidst voracious and sadistic expletives between the families. As a gunshot raced passed his head, Frank threw the door open to the outside and ran for his life. He knew that the trap would detonate at any moment.

The streams of stinging sweat ran down his forehead and were now starting to blind him as he blinked them away and continued his sprint. The furious sounds of the gun battle behind him echoed through the quiet city streets. I just need to get to the meeting spot, he kept thinking as he ran.

Rounding the corner at the end of the block, he saw his allies standing in the middle of the road, another block away. Fortunately, this area of the city had consisted of rundown warehouses that were abandoned and slated for demolition in the coming months. There was no traffic and no pedestrians to contend with, as per the plan.

He raced up the block and as he approached the guys, he screamed, "HIT IT! HIT IT!"

There stood Marcus and Detective Spinosa, aka John.

Once the detective had moved the skids of guns into the middle of the warehouse, he raced for his life out the side door and down the street to an awaiting Marcus.

Still out of breath, he now stood beside Marcus, who just stared past an advancing Frank to the warehouse in the background, with the remote detonator in hand. Revenge is sweet, he mused.

With one swift push of a button, the landscape became ablaze with fire and fury as the warehouse, filled with the notorious drug clans, exploded high into the sky. The three of them stood mesmerized by the bursts of flames that rose into the awaiting night sky. The synchronization of the flames was captivating.

After a silent second, Marcus, Detective Spinosa and Frank turned and confidently strode up the street together. Sirens began to scream in the distance. The trio weren`t worried about survivors. Detective Spinosa had informed the local police and fire departments about the bold takedown that was going to occur. In support of their fallen comrades to these drug families over the past years, these departments immediately decided that they would be acting with `slower-than-normal` response that day.

The threesome walked down the street as snow flurries started to swirl around their ankles. Each one of them silently reflected on their own personal justices that had just played out.

Marcus, walking in between the two, put a supportive arm around each guy as they continued ahead on their new journey.

CHAPTER THIRTY-TWO

The sunset the day after the explosions had been the most spectacular sight of his life thus far. Sitting on the edge of the over-sized boulders that lined the Hudson waterway, Marcus reflected on the happenings of the past 24 hours. He managed a faint smile, knowing that happiness was now within his reach.

He had accomplished what he needed to, but he would always have one nagging regret – that he had to leave Paige behind. He was determined to go back to try to find her, but was unsure if she would actually still be waiting for him. Right now, though, he needed to focus on reuniting with his family.

Still deep in thought and reflection, Marcus didn't hear the approaching foot steps behind him, and was startled when Detective Spinosa sat down on the rock beside him.

Not a word passed between them, as they stared at the picturesque sunset for a few minutes. With the bright red and orange colors reflecting off the Hudson River, Marcus' gaze remained glued to the now silent docks on the other side.

"Did Frank make it out okay?" Marcus asked in a quiet voice.

The Detective smiled, still staring straight ahead. "Yeah, I've been told that he's already on the beach with a Corona in one hand and a Brazilian beauty in the other. He'll be just fine down there," he replied with a laugh.

"How are you, Marcus? Are you going be okay?"

Marcus looked ahead solemnly. "Yeah. Obviously I have some very important calls to make to my family, and I'll have to start up my career again, but, yeah, I'll be fine."

He then looked over at the Detective and their eyes met for the first time since the take down of the families the night before. Still seeing sadness in Marcus' eyes, Spinosa decided it was time to reveal the guest he had brought along with him.

The Detective pointed over his shoulder. "Take a look. It's your turn to be happy, Marcus."

Without getting up, Marcus pivoted on the large rocks until he could see what Spinosa was referencing.   At the river's edge was a woman, her blonde hair catching the light of the sunset. It was Paige! He leaped off the rocks and ran straight into her open arms.

They held each other tightly, unable to speak, overwhelmed by emotion.

After a moment, he stood back and gently braced her shoulders so he could take a look at her angelic face. Marcus thought she had never looked as beautiful as she did at that moment.

"How...how did you find me?" he whispered. Paige, beaming despite the tears, looked at Spinosa, still sitting on the rocks, seizing up their embrace with a look of total satisfaction on his face.

"He arranged everything," she confessed in muted tones, before cracking the most adorable smile. "Besides, I got tired of waiting for you at the top of Nakiska. The view isn't the same without you!"

Marcus grinned at Spinosa and mouthed "thanks" and then cupped Paige's face in his hands. The kiss that followed was filled with the same passion they had once shared amongst the mountains.

He had reconnected with the love of his life. Now there was only one more thing to do to make his new life complete.

With one arm still around Paige's waist, he flipped open his cell phone and slowly thumbed in some numbers and switched it to speaker. After what seemed like forever, a kind, female voice answered tentatively, "Hello."

Marcus spoke soothingly, "Mamma...it's me – Marcus. I'm alive..."